And
Began to wonder

A writer's life in lockdown - 31
days - 31 stories

LAURA BILLINGHAM

Green Cat Books

Published in 2020 by
GREEN CAT BOOKS

19 St Christopher's Way
Pride Park
Derby
DE24 8JY
www.green-cat.co

ISBN: 978-1-913794-13-2

Although this book has been thoroughly proofread by
Green Cat Books, the author has chosen to omit some
punctuation.

DEDICATION

This collection of short stories is dedicated to all those who have supported me in my life.

In particular my mum and dad, who sadly both passed away just before we were all plunged into Lockdown Part 1.

A special mention to my daughters, Beth and Abbie and to my partner Grey – three people I can rely on to be there if I need them.

2020 may not have been the year any of us hoped for, but this collection of stories shows that out of trial and tribulation good things can emerge.

Laura Billingham

CONTENTS

1	And The Crows Began to Wonder	Pg 1
2	Different Strokes	Pg 7
3	Be Careful What You Wish For	Pg 15
4	Best Laid Plans	Pg 25
5	Where Am I?	Pg 35
6	Kinship	Pg 45
7	Stuck on Repeat	Pg 55
8	Me Time	Pg 63
9	Resistance	Pg 71
10	Beware The Beast	Pg 79
11	The Winning Game	Pg 89

CONTENTS

12 Spin Back   Pg 97

13 I Can Do This   Pg 107

14 Starry, Starry Night   Pg 115

15 Once Upon A Time   Pg 121

16 The Cat That Got All The Cream   Pg 133

17 Evolution   Pg 141

18 Time For Tea   Pg 143

19 New Age Order   Pg 151

20 How Special Am I?   Pg 157

21   Blood Ties   Pg 165

CONTENTS

22 Survivor   Pg 173

23 Just One Of Those Days   Pg 181

24 Human Being Not Human Doing   Pg 189

25 Blood Eagle   Pg 197

26 It's All Just Energy   Pg 205

27 Looking Ahead   Pg 213

28 A Parable For Our Times   Pg 221

29 Dystopia Falling   Pg 227

30 Expect The Unexpected   Pg 237

31 A Slip In Time   Pg 247

ACKNOWLEDGEMENTS

Thanks to all the people on my Facebook page who provided the prompts which let to each story's creation.

A particular shout out to Elaine Mitchell for two prompts – one of which allowed me to shape a story around our shared belief that 'everything is energy'!

Thank you to Pixie Drew (aka Nicola Holmshaw) for the cover design and for the amazing pencil sketches you will find at the top of each story. It's been a pleasure working with you again. Finally, thanks to Lisa Greener at Green Cat Books for taking on this project at such short notice!

1 May – from a prompt "and the crows began to wonder"

And the Crows Began to Wonder

It all began with a rumour.

No one knew where it had started…

A new virus.

A highly contagious virus.

Fuelled by social media the rumour spread around the world, but initially no one seemed to pay much heed.

Until…all around the globe people started to die. Old. Young. Fit and healthy. Weak and ill. The disease appeared to be indiscriminate.

The virus, if indeed that's what it was, produced different symptoms in different people and not everyone became infected...the medics of the world were baffled. None of their tests, their science, their accumulated knowledge was able to work out why and how people were dying.

Governments ordered their citizens into quarantine. Jobs were lost, businesses failed, economies began to falter but people, for the most part, abided by the lockdowns. Yet the deaths continued; in fact they accelerated.

In one day, some five months after the rumour first started, two million deaths were recorded.

The crows and all the other birds began to wonder ... "What happened to all the people?" They sat in their lofty nests chattering between themselves and gazing down at the empty roads, cities and villages.

The more curious of the crows ventured into the human areas, peering through windows, tapping on the glass for attention. Heads cocked on one side, they spied the people in their homes, as they huddled around the shiny screens with the moving pictures.

'Caw. Caw.' They crowed at the humans who gazed blankly back at them through the shield of their windows but made no attempt to make contact.

The crows shook their heads, flapped their wings and hopped up and down but the humans weren't interested in anything other than the screens in their hands or in their rooms.

Exasperated, the crows returned to their nests and told the rest of the birds that the humans must be hibernating, that something was amiss.

The wise old trees in which the crows made their nests, picked up on the messages of their feathered occupants and they in turn passed on the news that humans were hibernating. Via leaf and stem, root and branch, all the trees in all the world learnt that humans were staying inside, that there was something wrong in the world of man.

The grasses and plants heard the news.

The animals that ate the plants and the trees and the grasses ingested the news.

Even the creatures in the sea became aware that there was something wrong with man.

The Earth drew a long deep breath and exhaled

S. L. O. W. L. Y. For the first time in a very long time, nothing sharp bored into her to extract the riches of her body. Nothing noxious poured into her streams, rivers and oceans. Nothing foul was pumped into the sky.

She rested.

At peace.

The grasses and plants and trees grew lush and thick, and the insects and animals feasted on the riches, whilst the birds and creatures who in turn devoured them, grew fat and healthy.

The streams and rivers and seas cleared and the fish, the dolphins and the whales rejoiced.

Curious animals ventured into cities to see humans captive behind the walls, doors and windows of the buildings. Places creatures would never normally visit became new playgrounds.

Devoid of the usual vehicles, tarmac roads became animal trails. Birds sang out loudly, proudly, their songs no longer drowned out by the buzz of humanity.

And still the humans died...and the screens they relied on finally went blank.

By month eight, 50% of humanity had succumbed to the virus...and then, as silently as it had started, the contagion stopped. No new deaths or infections were reported for over two months and all around the planet humans began to emerge from hibernation.

Cautiously at first...tentative steps out into a changed world.

Governments had fallen.

Economies collapsed.

This was a brave new world for the survivors.

Those that remained marvelled at the wonder of the planet, how being spared the iniquities inflicted by humankind for so many months had enabled a rebirth – a reset.

They breathed in the clean air, smiled at the antics of the animals and birds, wondered at the lush growth of plants and trees and grass and vowed to never again take the world and nature for granted. Never again to take more than the planet freely gave. Never again to assume ownership of Her and all Her gifts.

The remains of humanity tore down the factories.

Flattened the shopping malls, the banks, the high rises, the slums.

They reopened schools, libraries and places of learning.

They learned to live with the rhythm of the seasons.

No power other than that obtained via the sun, the wind, the waves and the rivers was permitted.

They respected the planet and all upon it and She rejoiced...

and the world flourished again.

2 May prompt – from a prompt 'Then I realised, I didn't like the person she had become'.

Different Strokes

You can be friends with someone for years and years – unquestioning friendship that sees you both through good times and bad.

I had such a friendship – her name was Cecile and we first met at primary school – it was 'love at first sight', in the way small children will often commit intensely to one another.

She was small, dark and dainty – olive skinned with deep brown eyes and wavy dark brown hair that belied her French ancestry. I on the other hand was blonde, with muddy blue eyes - the colour of a puddle on an overcast day as my mum used to say

– and, aged five I was already head and shoulders above most of my classmates.

It really was a case of opposites attracting and yet we became inseparable very quickly.

To me, Cecile was intriguing, mysterious, and therefore utterly captivating. She was an only child and lived with her parents in a large house in the 'posh' part of town. Her bedroom was an Aladdin's cave of delights to me...masses of toys, a wardrobe full of pretty dresses and drawers chock full of t-shirts and jumpers, all brand new.

I lived with my parents and four older siblings in an ex-council house on the fringes of the catchment area for the school. To say we were pushed for space was an understatement – I shared a room with two sisters, my two older brothers shared another tiny box room which had scarcely enough room for bunkbeds and my parents had the remaining bedroom.

New clothes were something I never had, having two older sisters meant I was the queen of the hand me downs. As for toys – well there was little enough money for food and essentials, so our playthings were all second hand or scavenged items. Still, as a family we were very happy, and our home was full of love and laughter.

Visiting Cecile's immaculate decorated and tidy home was a treat for me, a welcome place of refuge from my own loud, chaotic and ebullient home environment. When I stayed for tea, we sat at a dining table covered with a crisp white cloth and laid with matching cutlery and crockery. The food was 'fancy' and quite unlike anything I had ever eaten before.

Cecile rarely came to my house after school – there was simply no room and I think that even at that young age I was aware that she would not fit into my household. Now, looking back, the thought of her eating fish fingers and oven chips whilst sitting on the sofa is enough to make me chuckle!

As we grew older and headed to senior school our differences began to show a little more, I was allowed to hang out in the street with the other kids whereas Cecile was whisked away by her mother in their shiny new car (changed every year). We were still firm friends, but I was beginning to work out the inherent snobbery in her upbringing. I can still recall the day when I was about to knock on the front door of her house, my hand stopped mid-air by the shrill sound of Cecile's mother swearing like a steelworker – I was, to coin a phrase – gobsmacked. Composing myself, I did knock on the door which was opened by her mother, all sweetness and light and rounded vowels – inwardly I had grinned.

I never mentioned this episode to Cecile as I guessed she would be embarrassed by what I had overheard, it did however make me re-evaluate her homelife. The shiny new stuff, up to the minute décor and airs and graces were clearly a façade and her parents, well her mother at least, was likely as 'working class' as my family. My grandmother, had I told her about this, would have said Cecile's mum was 'all fur coat and no knickers'…up until that point I had never understood what she meant by that.

The pair of us – Cecile and I - were dubbed 'the odd couple' by the other pupils of the school but we stuck together through thick and thin (and occasional boyfriends) up until we reached the 5th year of senior school aged 16. I planned to go to a further education college to study 'something practical' at the behest of my parents, whilst Cecile was destined for 'A' levels and university. Looking back, I don't think either of us was enamoured by the choices imposed on us but we both knew better than to protest.

We began to lose touch from that point on, our lives changing in many ways. I studied at college, got the qualification and went on to work in a bank...the kind of 'steady job with prospects' my parents wanted for me. Whereas Cecile scraped through her 'A' Levels and then went onto uni to study fine art...heaven knows why as she was one of the least artistic souls I ever met.

We met up every so often, even went on a couple of girly holidays, but although we would have done anything for each other we never regained the close comradeship of childhood.

By the time we reached our mid-twenties Cecile had met a regular hooray Henry of a chap, public school boy, old boy's network – a thoroughly obnoxious individual whom I despised from the word go. Predictably her mother was thrilled, and a lavish extravaganza of a wedding was thrown – I was maid of honour, dressed in a hideous (well that's what I think now) 'Gone With the Wind' inspired gown and hat.

She moved to Surrey and led the cosseted life of a 'kept woman'. A couple of children followed, boys, who were shipped off to boarding school, like their father before them, as soon as was deemed socially acceptable. Harry and Simon were their names.

I on the other hand forged a career in the banking sector, I returned to studying and eventually gained an MBA. Marriage and children were put aside whilst I climbed the career ladder but eventually, I met and married a wonderful man in my thirties and had a daughter just after my 40th birthday.

Cecile, who had been conspicuously absent at my wedding ("a long-arranged cruise, darling – I'm afraid I can't cancel...say you understand,") visited me once I was back at home with my beautiful baby. With a pinched look to her face and wearing what was clearly a very expensive outfit, she perched uncomfortably on the edge of one of my deliciously squishy leather sofas.

"May I hold her?" she asked – I think because she thought that was the 'done' thing.

Carefully I passed Chloe to her, unfortunately my feisty child did not take well to being passed around like a parcel and promptly spat up all over Cecile's silk blouse. With a genuine look of distaste, the baby was handed back to me whilst Cecile dabbed ineffectually at the mark on her front.

The visit lasted less than an hour after that, whatever closeness we once shared had clearly disappeared completely. Our life paths had diverged completely and I realised I didn't like the person she had become...the snobbery she had been brought up with had gone into overdrive and I no longer fit her idea of a friend.

These days we share Christmas and birthday cards at most – her husband is now in The House of Lords, having inherited some title or other, and Cecile swans around like lady muck. I still recall our early friendship with much fondness though – I wonder if she does?

3 May – prompt "be careful what you wish for"

Be Careful What You Wish For!

Have you ever noticed how when you long for something, when you've wished and dreamed about something that, when you actually have whatever it is, you feel a little deflated, disappointed even?

For years Maria had longed for an opportunity to get away from the job she loathed. She yearned for romance, excitement, a fulfilling career but instead she got up every day, dressed in the same uniform and went off to serve burgers and chicken nuggets to the great unwashed.

In her head Maria was a travel writer, flitting around the world staying in glamorous hotels and sending back sparking copy and stunning photographs to her handsome editor. The fact that she had barely scraped through her GCSE in English and didn't know one end of a camera from the other were things she glossed over. She daydreamed many a shift away imagining the exotic locations she would be assigned to and the gorgeous men she would attract.

Lost in one of these dreams, she was abruptly pulled back to real life by the sound of her supervisor bellowing her name.

"Maria! How many times have you been told not to leave the fryer unattended?!"

Shaking herself from her reverie – she'd been sipping a cocktail with a businessman called Mark, in a swanky hotel in Rio – she hurried to the fryer where her supervisor, practically incandescent with rage, was taking out basketfuls of fries. Far from being a uniform golden colour, these particularly potato snacks were a dark crozzled brown – so overcooked that they were hard and brittle.

Flushed with embarrassment she hurried to assist. In doing so she slipped on some spilled grease on the floor and cannoned into the supervisor knocking the basket he was holding into the scalding fat. With a loud expletive he pulled his hand back, a large red welt across the back of it indicating that some of the hot fat had burned him – quite badly by the look of it.

Mortified, Maria tried to help but he was having none of it. "Just bloody go!" he raged. "We're going to have to shut anyway as that fryer will need to be drained and cleaned to get rid of the burned smell. In fact, don't come back tomorrow either, take this as a final warning – I'll put it in writing later…if I can use my sodding hand, that is!"

Tears stinging her eyes - or was it the acrid smell of overheated fat and burnt fries? - she rushed into the room where the staff were allowed to keep their coats and bags whilst on shift. Without saying anything she donned her coat, picked up her shoulder bag and left via the back door.

Back at home, a dingy flat above a newsagents, she poured herself a large glass of a cheap white wine she'd picked up from the shop below and sat disconsolately on the shabby sofa.

For all the wishing to leave the job in the fast food shop, she hadn't ever really thought she would escape. Jobs weren't easy to come by and she'd never seriously thought John, the supervisor, would actually hold true to his word and sack her. True, she'd been given numerous warnings (she'd lost count) but he had never followed through with any of his threats and had never uttered the words 'final warning' before.

Taking a large gulp of the wine (and shuddering as it really wasn't very good) she sat back and stared up at the ceiling, what was she going to do?

She hauled her laptop out from under the sofa where she'd left it after creating a profile on an online dating site...the men who frequented the fast food joint left something to be desired, so she thought she'd take a chance on the internet.

"First things first," she muttered to herself and logged onto her bank account. What she saw there was not encouraging, assuming she would still get this week's money and payment in lieu of notice (she wasn't sure about that part) there was barely enough money to pay the rent which was due next week.

As she logged out of the banking site the machine 'pinged' and an email notification flashed on the screen...from the dating site! Excited, Maria opened her Gmail account and saw an email headed 'We have great news! Mario wants to talk to you!'.

Mario!

Mario and Maria...sounds perfect she thought clicking the email which opened in a new window. A slightly blurry photo of a man with dark curly hair and dark eyes smiled at her- Mario! She clicked the link to the dating site to look at his profile and read the message. A banner ad flashed up – 'Become a paid member to meet your matches'. Buggeration, she'd forgotten that part. Biting her lip in recollection of the parlous state of her bank balance, she clicked the pay now button anyway, entered her card details and was eventually able to see Mr Mario's details.

He lived in Italy! Maria almost swooned with delight. The rest of the profile was a little vague, no age was listed but his description was delicious...6' 1" (although that part was actually in cm so she'd had to check on Google); brown eyes, brown hair, fit, loved sports, travelled a lot, a chef in the family restaurant. She was smitten even before reading his message...

'Maria, bellissima, beautiful lady. I see your picture and my heart takes a big jump. You are so pretty I long to see you. Please answer to this message so we can talk more'.

Wow! Perhaps her luck was changing.

'Dear Mario,' she began, 'you are very handsome. I would love to talk to you. Here is my telephone number'. She paused at this point, was giving out her phone number sensible? 'Sod it', she thought, hurriedly typing the number. Before she could think about it any further, she hit the send button and closed the laptop. Done. For better or worse.

Several hours later after she'd drunk the rest of the bottle of wine, plus another she had remembered was in the back of a cupboard, her phone began to ring. Trying to focus on the number on the screen through alcohol glazed eyes proved tricky so she answered it anyway...

"Hello," she slurred.

A deep, heavily accented voice replied, "Ciao, Maria, eet is Mario I could not wait to speeek to you!"

Maria sat bolt upright, which made her head spin...Mario! She really hadn't thought he would call so soon – actually, she didn't really think he'd call at all.

A rather bitty conversation followed, not helped by his rather limited English, her complete lack of Italian and her drunken state. By the end of the conversation he was professing undying love and she was agreeing to go and visit him in Rome.

The next morning Maria woke up on the sofa, still fully clothed from the previous day and feeling like shit. Banging headache, mouth like the bottom of a hamster cage and a very queasy tummy.
"Urggghhh!" she groaned dragging herself into the bathroom where she promptly threw up.

It was gone midday before she recalled the conversation between her and Mario, had she really said she would visit him in Rome, and had he really said he would pay for a flight? A quick check of her emails revealed this was indeed the case and an E-ticket for a flight to Italy was already in her inbox. There were also numerous texts from Mario all saying he loved her and couldn't wait to see her.

Any sensible person would have pulled up short at this point and thought, 'no...' but Maria was not particularly sensible and, in any case had pined for such attention, not to mention travel, for such a long time. So, two days later she was boarding an Easyjet flight to Rome, hand luggage only.

Emerging into the busy arrival's lounge she spotted a sign with her name on being held aloft by a young man – not Mario, but she guessed he must be working in the restaurant. The young man was called Luigi and he explained he would take her to Mario and that his car was parked in the airport's car park. She dutifully followed along behind him and got into the tatty car he indicated; the drive itself was hair-raising and she was very glad when Luigi finally stopped outside a garishly lit pizza place.

"Mario's," he announced before picking up her bag and helping her out of the car.

With no further explanation he got back in the car and shot away.

Left standing on the pavement there was nothing Maria could do but go inside the brightly lit restaurant, only it wasn't really a restaurant she realised, more of a takeaway, not unlike the place she used to work in fact.

A middle-aged man, with salt and pepper hair that had probably once been dark brown, sporting a sizeable paunch and sweating profusely, was behind the counter. He wore a name badge pinned to his apron – 'Mario' it read.

Maria paled, surely this wasn't *the Mario*...nah, must be his dad, she thought.

The man noticed her at last..."Belissima! Maria!" he exclaimed. "You is heeer! Welcome." He popped open the counter and headed towards her, arms open wide.

She wanted to run, but where to? Strong arms surrounded her, holding her tightly. She inhaled the smell of sweat, garlic and pepperoni – a heady aroma that made her gag, yet at the same time want a pizza.

So, this WAS Mario! The man bore no resemblance to the blurry profile picture.

Three days later, having realised the plane ticket he had purchased was one way only, Maria stood next to a deep fat fryer in a burger joint near the airport – working to earn enough to pay for a flight back home. A phrase her mother often said rattled perpetually through her head…

'Be careful what you wish for'.

She'd wished for travel and romance. Had received both but neither was what she wanted!

4 May – prompt She left the house that morning, heart pounding, knowing this time she HAD to go through with it.

Best Laid Plans

She left the house that morning, heart pounding, knowing this time she HAD to go through with it. There could be no more procrastination, no more turning away – this was it.

As she walked towards the train station Julia mulled over the past few months...she didn't used to be so much of a procrastinator but recently she had seemed completely incapable of making any kind of decision – even choosing between tea or coffee in the morning was enough to throw her into a tizzy.

Julia's footsteps slowed as she neared the station, every step was bringing her closer to the ultimate destination and to the thing she had been avoiding for weeks – could she go through with this? Shaking herself she mentally recited a mantra someone had said could help… "You are strong. You are capable. You are amazing. You can do this." It did help, a little, and before she knew, she was on the platform waiting for the next train to the city.

Her usually immaculately coiffured hair was more 'au naturelle' than 'just stepped out of the salon' and her nails, usually painted a deep crimson were shorter than normal and varnish free. She still sported her trademark red lipstick – that was one thing she wouldn't want to give up – but the rest of her makeup was very subdued. She didn't look much like 'Julia Straker, ball breaker' and she knew it. A tiny, almost inaudible giggle escaped her as she imagined the reaction she'd get when she arrived.

The train pulled into the platform and a sudden rush of commuters surged to the opening doors, Julia hung back a little, not wanting to get caught in the scrum. Over the past four months she had relished peace and quiet and enjoyed the lack of hustle and bustle – this return to 'normal' actually felt like overwhelm and she felt her energy dip with the onslaught of so many people around her. With a sudden insight, Julia realised that she didn't enjoy this kind of environment one little bit and that realisation stiffened her resolve.

Boarding the rear carriage, she was fortunate enough to secure a seat and gratefully sat down, the journey wasn't particularly long – some 40 mins – but she was glad she wouldn't have to stand. She fished her phone and earbuds out of the capacious bag she carried and selected a calming soundtrack on Spotify – not only would it keep her stress level down but wearing the earbuds did tend to dissuade anyone from talking to her.

Julia had always been a very driven person, as a child she wanted to be top of the class and was never satisfied with anything other than straight A grades and coming first in every race and competition. Star performer she may have been, but it didn't exactly enamour her to classmates – the fact she was also incredibly attractive made her even less liked by the girls in the school. Boys found her knockout gorgeous but were so intimated by her that they tended to admire from afar rather than ask her out on a date.

If she hadn't been such a self-contained individual, she may have hated her school years, but the fact was, Julia didn't care much for what other people thought and neither was she particularly bothered by human interaction. School was simply a means to an end – good qualifications meant the best university and that was all she had cared about. She'd mapped out her life by the age of eleven and then went all out to follow her plan.

Arriving at Cambridge University aged eighteen had just been another step on her journey, she concentrated on getting her degree, bypassing entirely the 'fun' part of university living and graduated with a double First...much to her satisfaction and no one else's surprise.

If there was one hiccup along her planned route it was that she struggled to find a suitable job once her degree was over...roles in her chosen field were rather scarce. Not one to stay disheartened for long, Julia simply opted for a Master's degree and it was during those two years of her life that she stumbled upon a way to earn money – one she had never considered before.

It turned out that she was really rather good at

'playing the stock market', she appeared to have an inherent knack for spotting patterns and trends and buying/selling accordingly. By the end of her Master's degree she had accumulated a tidy amount of money (a six-figure sum) and with a suitable job still not apparent she took the bold step of sinking a great portion of that wealth into a start-up IT company.

Of course, this being Julia, she had done an enormous amount of research into the sector, the concept and the individual before handing over her cash AND she took up the role of CEO. Within 5 years, that start-up was turning over £25m a year, and the original 'ideas man' sold his shares to Julia...the company was now hers entirely and it continued to flourish. Her no-nonsense approach, solid business brain and fearless stance on innovation made the business the most successful in the sector and along the way earned her the 'ball breaker' nickname.

As the years went by and her 35th birthday was approaching, she began to grow ever more discontented with both the job and the glitzy lifestyle she was leading. Her original passion, the thing she had studied so hard at for 5 years, had been pushed out of her life. She managed however to keep up with new developments and maintained contact with people in the field and it was through one of those contacts she heard something that set her heart on fire.

Eighteen months of tests, trials and interviews followed – none of which were divulged to anyone in Straker Industries. Finally, just four months previously, she had received the news that would change her life forever - if she accepted.

The train had reached the final stop by now and Julia joined the hordes of commuters heading for their various places of work…had she really done this every day for more than 10 years? She picked up a black cab outside the station and directed it to the building which housed her company, the words 'Straker Industries' were emblazoned on the front. This central London office was merely the HQ and one of the 'knowledge' hubs, ten other offices were spread across the UK, US and China.

Paying the driver, Julia alighted and made her way to the glass front entrance – no going back now…she had been spotted by the doorman and the receptionist. Nodding to both and exchanging pleasantries she took the lift to the top floor where her office was located. It had panoramic views over the city and was, she thought, the only thing she would miss.

She had called the meeting of her top people around the globe for 2 p.m., meaning an early start for the those in the US and a late finish for the Chinese...they understood though, running a global business meant adapting to time zones. Her PA, Linda appeared and asked if she needed anything...waving her away, Julia simply asked her to ensure the video links for the meeting were good to go.

Fifteen minutes later the boardroom was filled with people and the large TV screen mirrored similar set ups in the other locations around the world. Once everyone was present Julia got to her feet...

"Team Straker – thanks all of you for attending this meeting. I'm sure you are all aware that I have been less present than usual in this business over the past several months and I now want to explain why."

People visible began to pay greater attention, sitting upright, leaning forwards...hanging on Julia's every word.

"I've built this company up from a tiny set up in a single roomed office, to the global enterprise it is today," Julia continued in a calm and measured voice. "But what most of you won't realise is that this business was not my original career path. I studied astrophysics for five years and that is my true passion, one I thought I would have to put aside for good." She paused and took a sip of water. "However, two years ago I was approached about a possible opportunity and I decided to pursue it without letting any of you know...basically because it was such a long shot and I didn't want to rock the boat here until I knew for sure."

Ripples of unease began to spread through the assembled groups...

"Well, now I do know – I have been selected to take part in the first manned mission to Mars...I am to be an astronaut!"

The various rooms erupted; this was not something anyone had seen coming. Shouts of congratulation could be heard above the general hubbub and Julia held her hand up to silence the commotion.

"Thank you all. Let me reassure you all that Straker Industries will continue. My legal team have been busy putting measures in place and my successor as CEO has already been approached and accepted the role. Ladies and gentlemen, let me introduce you to the new CEO of Straker Industries, Mike Walker." The gentleman in question rose and took a quick bow.

"All that remains for me to say is, I know you will continue to work as hard as you have always done and thank you for being such an amazing team!"

One year later, a very different Julia Straker boarded the vehicle that would take her and nine other intrepid individuals to Mars. None of them knew if they would ever return to Terra Firma but none of them really cared…they were doing what they knew in their hearts they were born to do.

5 May

<u>"Where am I?"</u>

That's the first thing I thought when I woke up...actually the thought was phrased in a rather more Anglo-Saxon way – if you know what I mean – but I edited it for the purpose of this story.

I digress...

I was in, or rather on as there didn't appear to be any coverings, some kind of bed. It wasn't particularly comfortable, yet neither was it uncomfortable – it just was. Cracking open one eye, I quickly shut it again as it seemed excessively bright. Forcing myself, I tried again, this time with both eyes, even though my lids seemed to stick together...

Damn! It WAS dazzling bright and my eyes watered in protest, wanting to immediately shut again of their own accord. I blinked rapidly, trying to acclimatise to the light and after a few seconds I was able to focus, although my eyes still watered.

It appeared that I was in a large room, I couldn't tell exactly how large because from my prone position I couldn't see the contours of the space...or so I thought. A moment later I realised that there actually seemed to be NO delineated edge to the walls, ceiling or floor. Everything was the same consistent, bright whiteness with no visible source of lighting – it was as if the entire room consisted solely of light.

Very bizarre.

I turned my attention to my body and performed a kind of mental inventory.

Legs: check. I could see them, move them, wiggle

my toes.

Torso: check. It was definitely there, and all seemed present and correct – and I was, I noticed both hungry and desperate for the loo!

Arms: check. I lifted first my right arm, then the left and waved them in the air. Fingers worked fine and my sense of touch was OK...the 'bed' I was on felt smooth, almost silky to my exploratory touch.

Head: check. My eyes were definitely functioning. "Helllllooo," I said aloud – yep, my voice and my ears were working too.

All good then, everything appeared to work as it should and no bits of me were missing or damaged...as far as I could tell.

Tentatively I drew myself up into a seated position, my head swimming alarmingly as I did; so much so that I almost flopped straight back down again. Curiosity won out over the dizziness though and I allowed myself a moment to quell the head spin before turning so that my legs hung over the side of the bed.

From this vantage point I could look around more easily. I was in some sort of space, bright white, no visible windows or doors and the floor, walls and ceiling all seemed to be made of the same material with no visible joins or marks anywhere. It was extremely disorientating – almost as if I were suspended in mid-air, there didn't seem to be 'a right way up'.

Throwing caution to the wind, I slid from the bed and onto the floor. Despite the clinical whiteness it wasn't cold underfoot, neither did it feel hard in the way of a tiled or concrete floor. It actually rather resembled the feel of a laminate floor with underfloor heating.

Feeling bizarrely buoyed up by this sense of the familiar, I tottered a little unsteadily towards the 'wall' directly in front of me and laid my hands against it. It too had a slight warmth to it and was, so far as I could tell, entirely smooth and unblemished. Thoroughly confused by this point I rested my head against the wall, only to immediately pull straight back...the wall was humming! Well that's the closest description I can provide of the noise – which stopped as soon as I moved my head.

I tried again, and, sure enough, as soon as I leaned my head back against the wall I could hear the same low resonant vibration. It was actually quite a soothing sound and so I let my head rest there for a while whilst I weighed up the situation.

The last thing I remembered before waking up here (wherever 'here' was) was getting into bed in my house in Sheffield. I was the only one in, everyone else having gone away for the weekend, and I was relishing the peace and quiet and looking forward to watching a sci-fi movie on Netflix whilst hoovering up a mountain of popcorn and drinking a bottle of wine. I remembered nodding off just after Han Solo was frozen in carbonite...and then - nothing.

Head still against the wall, I became aware of a slight change in the sound of the vibration. Suddenly there was a 'swishing' sound, a bit like the noise when you quickly draw the curtains, and I became aware of an 'opening' in the wall diagonally opposite me.

I span around pressing my back to the wall and waited to see if anyone (or anything?) would come through. Both petrified yet relieved...perhaps I was going to get some answers. I watched the opening expectantly and blinked in stupefaction at what I saw.

The person, for that was what walked through, was a stunningly attractive woman dressed in an ice blue gown which clung to her torso before flaring gently to just above her feet. Said feet were shod in boots of the exact same colour as the dress.

Her hair, worn unbound, was a silvery blonde which fell in waves to almost the small of her back, and her eyes were the clearest shade of blue I had ever seen – almost aquamarine. She didn't appear to be wearing any make-up, but her skin was a flawless golden shade, unblemished and devoid of any wrinkles.

"You look like I imagine an angel would," I blurted out.

The woman laughed, a beautiful tinkling sound. "Yes, we have indeed been called angels in your world...we don't have wings though!" She turned to show me the lack thereof.

"I am glad to see you are awake, Elena. You must have many questions for me, for us. My name is Senara, please, put this on." She held out her hand from which draped something the same shade of blue as her dress.

Until this point I had singularly failed to realise that I was clad in only the shorty pyjama set I'd put on for my 'big night in', a fact which gave me some relief...perhaps this was merely a dream and I'd wake up soon.

Senara glided over to me (well that's what it looked like). Close up, she was still flawlessly beautiful and she exuded a gentle sweet perfume. Meekly I took the item of clothing which turned out to be a robe, with a tie belt, and put it on – immediately I felt less vulnerable.

"How do you know my name?" I asked.

"We know many things about you and your kind Elena, but come – I'll answer all your questions once you have had a chance to eat and drink."

At the mention of food and drink I again became acutely aware of my need to go to the loo and, as if reading my mind, Senara added, "But first perhaps you would like to, how do you people say it...freshen up."

She waved a hand and another opening appeared in the wall, this time next to me. I peered in and spied a toilet – no further explanation was required from either of us.

A few minutes later, feeling mightily relieved (pun intended) I re-joined Senara, the 'door' had closed when I entered the bathroom and re-opened once I was done, so I assume there was some kind of sensor.

She smiled and beckoned me to follow her. As we walked along a white corridor (what is it with white I asked myself) Senara kept up a gentle dialogue, asking me questions about my favourite foods, drinks, likes, dislikes etc. and I found myself answering freely, any residual fear or tension dissipating as we walked. After a couple of minutes she stopped and placed her hand against the wall – I could see there was a slight difference in the shade and texture of the area she put her hand and assumed it was some sort of lock. A reasonable assumption as it turned out because another opening appeared with a gentle swish and we walked through.

This space contained a table, upon which was a platter bearing a selection of my favourite fruit, a smaller plate of what looked for all the world like buttered toast and a cup from which a curl of steam and an aroma of tea emerged. I glanced at Senara, I'd mentioned all of these things as we'd walked along – how had she done this?

The combined smell of tea and toast overrode any questions I had, and I gratefully demolished them both, and a banana, before saying anything.

Seeing I'd apparently eaten my fill, she beckoned for me to follow her to the other side of the room; I did so, still clutching the cup of tea which I hadn't quite finished. Senara said something that I either didn't quite catch or maybe didn't understand and suddenly the entire wall in front of us disappeared to be replaced with a vista of bright stars and a view of what looked like planet Earth.

My jaw dropped. As did the cup I'd been holding. What the actual fuck was going on?

Senara smiled at my confusion, "You aren't dreaming, that is your planet and we are looking at it from space. You're onboard a Pleiadean ship, my kind are watching, guarding if you will, your planet whilst it goes through a rebirth. It is our aim to act as midwife while Earth transforms to the next level of development."

I gazed blankly at her serenely beautiful face – what she said had made perfect sense at an instinctive gut level to me, in fact I'd been telling people for years that something big was happening, that the world was changing for the better.

"You're wondering why you're here?" I nodded and she continued. "Certain people, and you are one of them are, on a cellular level, aware what is happening. Your planet is finally awakening from the darkness and transcending to the 5th dimension. People like you need to know that your kind is not alone and that you are supported. That is why you are here. We don't expect you to share this knowledge that the Pleiadeans and other star people are watching and silently helping…it is enough that sufficient numbers of you are aware."

It was as if a switch had been flicked inside me – I knew, I absolutely knew and understood what she meant, and I nodded my head. I'd always known, deep inside, that this day would come – it was if I had waited my entire life for validation of what I already knew.

Senara took my head in both hands and kissed me lightly on the forehead over my 'third eye'. "You will be safe," was all she said before I felt consciousness leaving me.

Stretching, I opened my eyes to find I was back in my own bed. The TV was still on but The Empire Strikes Back had long since finished and instead the Netflix carousel of images was flicking round.

I didn't question if I had just dreamt what had happened – I knew it had and I was at peace… change was coming but I was ready for it.

6 May from prompt "the paper slowly drifted from her cold hand"

<u>Kinship</u>

Fee wasn't sure when she had first realised she was different. From a very young age she was aware of being able to 'do' things that other people couldn't, but she'd never put a name to her powers.

Adopted as a small child by a God-fearing couple and denied access to any of her kin (not that she knew if she had any blood relatives) she had learned very early on to hide anything out of the ordinary. The first (and only) time she had said anything at all to her adoptive parents about her unusual abilities, had resulted in no supper for a week and extra chores. As they berated her for her 'unnatural powers', Fee had the feeling that if they could have beaten them out of her, they would.

To keep the peace, she promised never to use her abilities again. She kept her mouth shut and was careful never to do anything which may lead her parents to believe she was still using her gifts.

In private of course, she delighted in using magick...just in small inconsequential ways; like levitating and floating around her room or calling for things to come to her when she felt too lazy to get up and get them. She wasn't really sure how exactly her power worked; with no one to talk to or learn from, she simply made things up as she went along. If she wanted to fly, she just thought about it and it happened. When she wanted an object to come to her, she commanded it to...it was as simple as that.

Her parents had moved towns when they adopted her – 'for a new start' they told her when she asked why. When she was old enough to understand, Fee reckoned they had moved because everyone in the old neighbourhood had known they had adopted a child rather than produce one themselves. She was wrong on that count - they actually wanted to keep her from her past.

Keen to obliterate any trace of magick, or at least bury it so deep that it didn't resurface, they dragged Fee to church every Sunday, enrolled her in Sunday school and sent her to a church-run school. Religion was thrust upon her at every occasion. She simply absorbed all the good parts: be kind, be good, love thy neighbour; ignored all the bad bits: sexism, homophobia, hypocrisy, and kept right on doing her magick.

As she grew older she realised that her parents were scared of her, not because they realised what she could do – she'd been far too careful to hide her abilities after that first occasion – but because of what they knew about her past. She didn't know how she knew that; they never spoke to her about her life before she was adopted aged 4, but somehow she did. Sometimes she would catch them looking at her and then at each other, a wary look in their eyes.

Their unease grew the older she got, fuelled perhaps by the fact that as she passed puberty she developed into a strikingly attractive young woman. Dark, almost black, curly hair framed a heart shaped face, almond shaped hazel-green eyes fringed with long black eyelashes were set above a small straight nose and full rosy lips. Physically she was the complete opposite of her adoptive parents in every way; they were tall, she barely topped 5'4"; they were bulky and out of shape, she was lithe and strong; they were blonde, she was dark.

It was inevitable that comparisons were drawn by outsiders. When the three of them were seen together people would nod knowingly to each other and Fee's adoptive parents became paranoid about appearing in public with her. This suited her down to the ground as they stopped wanting her to accompany them everywhere, especially church, and left her more or less to her own devices. One day just after her eighteenth birthday, which had barely been acknowledged let alone celebrated, Fee, on a whim decided to catch a bus to the nearest big city. To the best of her knowledge she had never visited there before, but as the bus drew closer to the centre, she began to experience a very strong sense of déjà vu.

The tiny hairs on the back of her neck began to prickle and she felt a tingle down her spine. Although she had planned to journey right into the main bus station in the city centre, she found herself pressing the bell to halt the bus as it passed through an outlying suburb. Almost in a trance, Fee jumped from the bus and stopped to watch it pull away. She was standing outside a line of three shops – a newsagent, proudly proclaiming it sold National Lottery tickets; a hairdresser and the one she was directly in front of. This particular shop had paintwork the colour of the sky, at the deepest darkest part of the night, accented by a trim of metallic silver. The sign above the window read 'Witch Way is Up' and the window display was a mish mash of dream catchers, crystals and other random esoterica.

Fee was charmed and pushed open the door eager to have a browse around the types of objects her adoptive parents would have a blue fit about, calling them 'the work of the devil'. A pleasant tinkling bell sound announced her arrival into the shop which appeared to be empty apart from herself. As she was cursorily examining a haphazard stack of books, a voice emerged from the recess of the shop causing her to jump and knock over the pile.

"Bugger!" she exclaimed, falling to her knees to gather up the scattered volumes.

"No need to fuss my dear, here, let me help you."

Fee turned her head and spied a woman, perhaps in her early 40s, long dark hair loosely plaited, wearing a voluminous purple dress which reached to her ankles. She was smiling widely and her dark eyes crinkled at the corners, this was a woman who embraced laughter if the tracery of fine lines around her eyes were anything to go by. As she reached Fee however, her expression changed to one of shocked recognition.

"It can't be! Come here, let me see you properly!" The woman stretched out a hand and lightly cupped the side of Fee's face causing a tingle, almost like a mild electric shock, to pass through her.

"Fee!" It wasn't a question. "Oh, my dear, I never thought I would see you again!"

Rising to her feet, a shocked Fee faced the stranger, who didn't *feel* like a stranger in the slightest. They were exactly the same height and their eyes connected immediately; Fee felt a tremor of recognition herself.

"Mum?" Although only just four when she'd been adopted, she still vaguely remembered a pretty woman with dark eyes telling her stories and rocking her to sleep.

The older woman nodded, eyes glassy with tears. "I should have guessed you would find your way here eventually. They told me never to look for you, but I suppose they didn't count on the bond we have and that you'd come looking for me!"

"But I wasn't looking for you, at least I don't think I was – I just needed to get away from my parents. Their house makes me so claustrophobic. I was heading for the city centre, but something made me get off here…OH!" The penny dropped. "It was YOU!"

"Well not just me," the other woman said. "When they took you from me I cast a bonding spell over both of us. It meant that if ever we were near each other we would find a way to meet. I'd lost hope of that happening if I'm honest – fourteen years is a long time, I worried the spell had lost its magick. Speaking of which…"

Fee smiled, "Yes, I can do some!" she said, allowing herself to levitate, just enough so that she was raised above her mum. "We have a lot to catch up on I think!"

None of this felt at all strange to Fee, in fact, just the opposite, for the first time that she could remember she felt at ease with herself and her surroundings… she felt accepted for who and what she was. But she had questions.

Her mother headed for the shop door, locked it and turned the sign to 'closed', her face was wreathed in smiles. "Come, I need to show you something."

Fee followed her through the door at the rear of the shop and up a steep flight of stairs to what was obviously the living accommodation. The space was small but spick and span, the walls were painted white and adorned with colourful mandalas and exquisite images of plants and trees, whilst crystals were strewn across the windowsill. She took a seat on the single sofa which was draped in a soft throw covered in colourful representations of the 'tree of life' – it was a beautiful room and one in which she felt right at home.

Her mother, and she knew beyond doubt this WAS her mother, disappeared into another room and returned seconds later carrying a wooden box. Sitting down next to Fee she told her a story which was both shocking and yet rang very true. She explained that her 'adoptive parents' had in fact snatched Fee when she was not quite four years old (the day before her birthday in fact) and threatened her mother with all sorts of retribution if she had tried to find them. They were devout Christians, vehemently opposed to anything they considered Pagan, and they had been utterly convinced that she was a devil worshipper who was leading her daughter along a path of evil.

Fee was dumbstruck – what had given them the right to take her? She was chilled to the core...what could they have threatened her mother with to keep them apart all these years. She had to ask.

In response to the question, her mother handed her a single piece of paper. Fee recognised the handwriting – her adopted father's. The note read, 'Miriam, we have taken your daughter Fee. It is an abomination to us that one so innocent is being raised to worship Satan. We have saved her from you and your master and will raise her as our own. If you try to get her back we will have no option but to take her life and return her soul to God to save her from your evilness.'

Fee watched as the paper slowly drifted down from her cold hand to the floor. Her gut told her that he had meant every word of that chilling message – they would have killed her if her mother had tried to find her. To them that would have been mercy, not murder.

Miriam hugged her daughter. She had hoped against hope that Fee would find her, that the magick which was part of her lineage and her birthright would have survived – and it clearly had...they could start her training now – training that would see Fee join the others around the world silently fighting to keep light in the world.

7 May – prompt "good morning world"

Stuck on Repeat

"Good morning world!" Gemma threw open the shutters which opened on to the small balcony and stepped out into the fresh clean air. The sound of birds could be clearly heard and in the distance a lamb bleated, the plaintive cry quickly followed by a reassuring 'baaa', presumably from its attentive mother.

Taking several deep breaths, she raised her arms into the air and began her morning affirmations; a ritual she had first begun several weeks ago and which she was finding was the very best way to start the day on a good footing.

'I love living here!' she thought to herself. 'Best move I ever made'.

Rituals completed for the day, she headed to the bathroom for a shower where she luxuriated in the scent of the soap she'd bought online. Gemma was a great believer in online shopping – "it's what the internet was invented for" she was known to say, and she made most of her purchases that way. Not really a 'people' person, the anonymity of shopping via her laptop suited her down to the ground. Of course she had to face 'real shops' occasionally but she kept those encounters to a minimum.

Once showered and dressed in loose-fitting black yoga pants and a baggy t-shirt, she put a load of washing in the machine in her small utility room before heading to the kitchen.

"Hmmm...what shall I have for breakfast?" she asked herself out loud, before moving automatically to prepare what she always had...a cup of tea and a slice of buttered toast. This never varied, Gemma was a creature who thrived on routine, without it she entered panic mode.

Breakfast over, dishes washed, dried and put away and the kitchen cleaned and tidied, she headed for her workspace, a small desk in the corner of her living room. Gemma was an artist, she created amazing images using her computer and a linked drawing tablet. Her work was in great demand and often used by bands and musicians for the covers of their albums and CDs.

Lost as always in the joy of creating something beautiful, she was distracted by an annoying regular beep and the sound of voices, but she blocked her mind to the distraction and carried on working.

Lunchtime came and went but Gemma was lost in the piece of art she was working on, a complex mandala for the cover of a book she had been commissioned to undertake. The bright colours and intricate design were hypnotising, but eventually she had to break in order to rest her eyes. Stretching, she noticed the clock in the corner of her screen – it read 19.30…how had so much time passed without her noticing?

She decided to call a day to the working endeavour and go and find something to eat for supper. The cupboards in her immaculate kitchen were ordered; tins and packets were regimentally lined up – pasta – pesto – passata – rice – tuna. Gemma selected a packet of fusilli and a jar of pesto and within 10 minutes was seated on the sofa eating her meal.

She turned on the TV and clicked the Netflix option where she selected her favourite show, 'The Good Witch' — it was undemanding viewing...she thought of it as 'wallpaper' for her brain...it enabled her to relax, it's saccharine sweetness a balm to her busy mind.

Bedtime followed at around 10 p.m., as soon as her head hit the pillow she was asleep.

****

"Good morning world!" Gemma threw open the shutters which opened on to the small balcony and stepped out into the fresh clean air. The sound of birds could be clearly heard and in the distance a lamb bleated, the plaintive cry quickly followed by a reassuring 'baaa', presumably from its attentive mother.

****

"How long has she been like this?" A medic wearing head to toe PPE picked up the chart from the end of the bed in which a young woman lay surrounded by all the machines required to keep her functioning. The hissing of the oxygen supply and sighing and the steady beep of the heart monitor were the only things indicating that the woman was alive – she was still and motionless, her skin a pale creamy pallor.

"333 days," was the response from the ICU nurse who was accompanying this new doctor on his first ward round. "She came in with Covid-19 symptoms and rapidly deteriorated. We were able to take her off forced ventilation within 10 days, but she's never regained consciousness."

"Next of kin?" the doctor enquired.

"None that we've been able to trace so far; she lived by herself in a remote farmhouse, it's lucky she was even found. An Amazon delivery driver was concerned when she didn't answer the door, apparently she was a regular on his round. An almost total recluse from what we can establish, evidently not keen on people and got most of her supplies online it seems, so heaven knows how she got the virus!"

"Has an EEG been done? This is an excessively long time to remain in a persistent vegetative state."

"Not for several months – I'll sort one out now," replied the nurse, already picking up her phone.

Several hours later the patient was hooked up to

yet another machine; myriad wires ran from the electrodes fixed to her scalp to the EEG device on its portable trolley. A scritchy, scratchy sound could be heard as the trace moved over the paper.

The nurse who had ordered the test watched the trace for a few seconds, some movement would be expected even for a patient in a persistent vegetative state but this one looked 'normal'. She called over the doctor to show him.

"Odd! Yes, you're right, she's definitely not in a PSV. That doesn't even look like a dream state – it's as if she's actually awake. Let's get an MRI ordered to check there's no damage to the brain. If that shows no abnormality then we'll need to work out the best course of action going forwards."

****

Gemma sat at her desk working on the artwork for the album cover, but she couldn't concentrate. An exceptionally loud throbbing hum was distracting her making work impossible.

She stood up and walked to the balcony door, even the sound of birdsong and the bleating lamb was blotted out by the horrid humming. She shook her head hoping to be rid of the annoying sound but it persisted…

"Gemma! Gemma!" The sound of someone calling her name broke over the sound and she honed onto the new noise – anything but the hum!

"Gemma! You're OK, don't be frightened, you're in hospital in an MRI machine."

Gemma didn't recognise the voice and what it was saying made no sense, but she focussed on it all the same. The hum stopped abruptly. She opened her eyes, even though she had no memory of closing them, and was confronted by several worried looking people wearing hospital-style protective clothing.

"It's OK Gemma," said a male voice. "You're in hospital. Do you remember anything at all?"

She tried to speak, but her mouth was too dry so she simply shook her head. Hospital?! The last thing she recalled was not being able to work on her latest project.

The same voice spoke reassuringly to her. "Everything will be alright now, you've been in a coma for almost a year but it looks like we've got you back! We'll get you back on your feet and then you can head back to your lovely house in the countryside.

8 May – prompt "Why, after all this time, are you doing this now?"

Me Time

"Why, after all this time, are you doing this now?"

"Because I bloody can – that's why. Because for the first time in my life I don't need to answer to anyone. I can do what suits me because I want to do it – not because someone else needs or wants me to!"

Louise turned on her heel and marched out of the open plan kitchen diner, slamming the door behind her to underline her feelings. She hadn't expected her partner of 10 years to particularly like what she had just told him, but she had at least expected some understanding…just a smidgen, to show that he appreciated why she needed to do this. As she headed up the stairs to her office she heard his final plaintive words…

"But what about me?"

That was the final straw as far as she was concerned – all her life she had been expected to put other people's needs above her own. Society still pinned girls and women with the badge 'care giver' and the need to please everyone else, take care of others is drip fed into the psyche from an early age.

Louise had absorbed all these societal pressures, played by the rule book. She'd taken care of her sisters when they were small, looked after friends and colleagues and bent over backwards to be the perfect wife and mother. Where had all that got her? Divorced by the aged of 35 with two young children, because her husband assumed he could continue the single life of bars and clubs and leave her to look after the house, children and him without complaint. Left heartbroken aged 39, when the man she still considered the love of her life had dumped her saying he needed freedom – only to move in with another woman within six months. Then a mercifully brief marriage to a narcissist with a porn habit!

"No," she muttered under her breath, "this is my time now and he can bloody like it or lump it as can every bugger else."

She sat down at her desk and began to make a list of what she would need to do and buy before she could begin her adventure. It turned out to be a relatively short list once she realised she didn't actually need much at all. That revelation made her giggle internally – all the crap, baggage and belongings we think we need turn out to be just burdens once you strip back to basics. It was freeing to finally understand that at the end of the day most of the 'stuff' in her life was just that...'stuff'. And more than that, it was stuff she didn't actually need in order to be happy.

Louise began to assemble the clothes and other bits and pieces on her list – the top two items were laptop and Kindle...she could still write and indeed planned to document her activities on an ongoing basis.

The front door slammed, and she peered out of the window to see Peter standing in front of the source of her excitement and his frustration...the second-hand motorhome she'd bought with the proceeds from her first novel. He paced around it, kicked a couple of tyres and then tried the side door – it was locked of course. She knocked on the window and shouted, "Want to take a look?"

Peter turned to face the window and nodded, so she rose to her feet and headed downstairs, keys in hand.

She knew that, as a practical man, Peter needed to examine the vehicle she had already christened 'Bessie'. His world was very much a physical one and he had little time for flights of fancy or anything intangible.

Louise unlocked the side door into the accommodation part of the vehicle; it was only a two berth, so the space was compact but thoughtfully laid out and was actually quite stylish...he seemed impressed, but determined not to show it.

"Bit small," he grunted. "I'd struggle."

"Yes, you probably would," Louise responded, "which is why I'm going on my own!"

"Hrrmmph!" It sounded as if he was clearing his throat. "Let's have a look at the cab."

The cab, as he called it, wasn't separate from the accommodation and had two seats which swivelled towards the living space when not actually being driven.

"Automatic," he nodded approvingly. "That'll make it easier for you to drive. Is it diesel?"

Louise nodded her head.

"Good, only five and a half thou' on the clock too. Well I have to confess it is much better than I thought Louise, I may even be tempted to give it a try."

Louise's heart sank – part of her was relieved that he seemed to be coming around to the concept of the motorhome, the other was worried that he may want to come with her!

"I'm glad you can see how beautiful Bessie is, and I hope one day you will come on a trip in her, but the next three months are just for me. It's not that I don't love you Peter, it's just I need some time for me. Some time when I'm not constantly thinking about what someone else needs. Some time when if I want to do nothing but sit and stare into space I can, knowing that I won't be interrupted, or have to make dinner, or – well – even speak to anyone!"

Peter looked defeated and slumped onto the seat on the passenger side of Bessie.

"Your mind is made up isn't it?" She nodded. "What am I supposed to do when you're gallivanting around Ireland?"

She felt her ire begin to rise again. "Anything you bloody well like! That's the whole fecking point of this, for me at least. We don't have to live in each other's pockets Peter, some time apart may actually be very good for us, don't you see that?"

"I see that you may decide you don't want to be with me anymore!"

"I could decide that anyway, irrespective of whether I take this trip." Louise almost shouted in response to his continued whinging. "I need to give ME a chance just to be ME for a while and if you don't understand that, understand me, then perhaps we shouldn't be together!"

That shocked him, you could see by the way his jaw clenched and unclenched. She was tempted to reassure him, but she was realising that this was his problem - not hers and so she said nothing at all. Finally, after a couple of minutes, during which time you could almost hear the cogs in his mind turning he said, "When will you go?"

'Hoo-bloody-ray', Louise thought, mentally punching the air, "Two weeks tomorrow, I need to do a spot more research and highlight the areas I should visit. My editor also needs an outline of the proposed book so I must do that too."

He sighed, "You're an impossible bloody woman at times, you know that Louise? But I wouldn't swap you for the world. Bugger off and do this then, I know you don't need and probably don't want my blessing, but you have it anyway. And maybe once you're back we can look at taking Bessie on a trip together – as long as we can get an awning so I can at least have somewhere to stand up straight!"

Louise laughed, "Aye, OK, I think that could be arranged! Now do you think you could help with an itinerary?"

"My pleasure…but how about you take me out for a spin in Bessie? I'll treat you to fish and chips on the way back and we can christen the dining table!"

"You're on!" she said jumping into the driving seat and firing up the engine, "Let Louise's adventures in Bessie begin!"

"Tallyho!" laughed Peter as they set off, harmony restored, and a new deeper understanding between the two of them forged.

9 May, prompt "After the announcement, a deathly silence fell over the room and a few people felt a shudder run down their spine."

<u>Resistance</u>

After the announcement, a deathly silence fell over the room and a few people felt a shudder run down their spine.

It was one thing hearing the news second-hand, but actually having someone in front of you was different entirely...it somehow made things more real.

The first inkling that something, or someone, was on the way to planet Earth had begun to emerge only a month or so ago, when roughly one in ten of the global population began to have extremely vivid dreams. Dreams of huge pyramidal shaped crafts appearing above their heads; of fair haired, golden-skinned beings speaking to them – warning them, preparing them.

Then reports of disappearances began to filter through to the mainstream press – although the reports were quickly refuted after the initial excitement. First, just one or two people and then ten or more at a time. Sometimes the taken reappeared but they had no memory of where they had been or what had happened to them.

Governments around the world accused the media of whipping up hysteria – there was, they said absolutely no evidence of anything at all out of the ordinary. They said no one should worry, that it was just the media creating the furore. To prevent any further spread of panic caused by 'disinformation', all further reporting of incidents was banned.

Most people didn't believe their elected (or enforced) representatives, choosing instead to go with the evidence of their own eyes. Strange things were happening; lights moving rapidly through the sky, mutilated cattle and other animals, bizarre weather and odd cloud formations were common.

Eventually groups of those who had experienced the most vivid dreams banded together and began to document what they had seen. The consistency was incredible – their stories were identical, warning of a threat to humanity coming from the INSIDE – from those already in power, with the support of their extra-terrestrial overlords. The golden-skinned beings transmitting the warnings were delegates from another star race. One which had been battling for millennia to rid the galaxy of the dark influence of the very entities now effectively running planet Earth.

Finding that their messages were quickly taken down if posted via the internet, unable to get onto reputable TV stations - effectively banned from ALL media sources, the messengers took to word of mouth dissemination via small 'social' gatherings. It was hoped that the powers that be would be unable to identify such gatherings and so the message could be communicated far and wide.

This was one such meeting, about twenty people were gathered in a local bar, ostensibly celebrating the successful completion of a course of study. In reality all were part of a resistance type group, eager to hear what the warnings to humanity actually were.

The key speaker, the one who had caused the spinal shudders, was a former cabinet minister in the current government who had been pushed out in a reshuffle but had been present when sensitive information had been discussed. They were risking a charge of treason for breaking the official secrets act by sharing information with non-government officials.

After she confirmed what most of the assembled group already knew, she went further to say that the leader of the so-called free world, the US president, plus the UK prime minister and the Russian president were in fact aliens adopting human form. She also suspected that the leaders of North Korea, India, Australia, Sweden and several other countries around the world were also alien infiltrators.

There was uproar in the room...how could she be sure? The politician explained that she had personally witnessed the UK prime minister struggling to maintain human form, how sometimes in a cabinet meeting he would appear 'fuzzy round the edges' and appear to morph into a reptilian persona for a split second. She said that most people appeared not to notice; and that oddly it was only the women who would look at each other bemused whenever it happened.

"What is their objective?" someone in the room asked.

"Dominion," said another voice.

"Control," added another.

"Both," said a third. "The aim is to destabilise this planet so that Earth cannot ascend to the 5th dimension as had been prophesised it will during this time period."

Another voice added, "But why does this matter?"

Suddenly the room was illuminated with a bright golden light, so dazzling that many of the occupants were forced to shield their eyes until they became accustomed to the glare.

A shimmering form appeared before them...

"It matters because Earth has become the battle-ground betwixt dark and light. It was prophesised millennia ago and this prophesy is now being played out. We, the guardians of the light have been watching for thousands of years, waiting for this moment – the tipping point in the galactic struggle."

A ripple of recognition of this truth sped around the room.

"Your leaders are pushing their truths at the behest of the dark forces. These constructs of dark are determined your planet will follow the descent into despair as others have done before. They thrive on deceit, on competition, on mastery of the masses and obscure the truth for their own benefit. When questioned on their many failings they, will deny any culpability, any responsibility."

Around the room heads were nodding.

"What can we do?"

"Hold the light," the visitation said. "All around your planet your people are waking up, realising and recognising that there is another way. Stay strong, stay focused – you are so very nearly at the tipping point. Keep the momentum going. Keep questioning. Keep your intentions and your vibrations high. Do not allow the few to subjugate the many. I and many like me are surrounding the Earth now, using our vibrations to help keep yours high and growing higher. We will not desert you. You will prevail."

The golden image blinked out, plunging the room

into relative darkness again. An excited hubbub filled the air. People chatted, compared notes but not one of them was in the least bit surprised by what appeared to have been an alien visitation. On the contrary, everyone was completely at ease – as if in their hearts and minds they had been expecting it.

And so the fightback against the dark began, not with weapons and wars but with ordinary people refusing to bow to the dictates of their dark leaders. No one raised a fist in anger, no one marched or protested and there were no revolutions. Instead, people went about their business quietly and with dignity. They shared, they loved, they built up their communities.

Slowly but surely the vibration of the planet grew too high, too pure for the dark reptilian forces and they began to lose their grip on power. Governments tumbled without the backing of their overlords and new representative bodies were created. Power for the people, by the people.

Wealth was redistributed as those that held the most fell with the rest of the dark ones. Art and beauty, love and kindness became the currency of the new world and as the last of the old collapsed, the star beings made themselves known to all humanity and Earth was welcomed back into the Galactic community.

Earth became a New Eden for all its inhabitants and a new Golden Age began.

10 May – prompt "just keep running as far and as fast as you can"

Beware the Beast

It was late and I was tired, very tired, that kind of deep in the bones weariness that makes you just want to drop whatever it is you are doing, curl up and go to sleep. I couldn't do that unfortunately as I had to keep on loading up the sand crawler before giving into rest.

Once the sun set on this planet it was no longer safe to stay out in the open and I had already lingered too long before beginning to pack everything away.

Finally, with a last surge of energy, I heaved the last box of scientific instruments into its prescribed spot in the loading bay and jumped in after it. It was fully dark now, the rocky landscape changed from the daytime reddish hue to a shadowy grey blue. Stars pricked the black canopy of the sky and twin slivers of moons were just becoming visible.

Sighing with relief, I sloughed the heavy boots and cumbersome, yet protective jacket and trousers. In contrast to the chill outside, the interior of my sand crawler was warm and toastie as the heat stored from the sun during the day was released back into the compartment.

I looked around the space I had called 'home' for the last eight weeks. It was small but contained everything a single person required during a spell surveying this new planet – even a small shower which I headed towards, shedding my remaining clothes as I did so. As an introvert I really enjoyed the opportunity to spend time on my own and absolutely relished the sheer joy and freedom of being able to pad around naked once the day's work was done. Letting the warm water sluice away the sweat and red dust from my skin and hair, I giggled as I imagined wandering around nude back at base camp…it would definitely be frowned upon.

Clean at last, I took a dry micro towel from a pile on a shelf next to the toilet and shook it out; from a 10cm square it expanded into a towel that wrapped comfortably around me. I shook my hair to rid it of a little of the water and then pulled a comb through it, I kept it short when on mission and it was ready for cutting; for a moment I considered fetching a pair of scissors and tackling it myself but thought better of it.

Using my hand to clear the condensation from the small mirror I contemplated my face...large blue eyes stared back – definitely my best feature. Sandy coloured hair stuck up in all directions and a band of freckles crossed from cheekbone to cheekbone across my stubby nose. A generous mouth and small chin completed my face – I was, I thought to myself, definitely no beauty. And yet there was an openness and lack of vanity to me that others appeared to find attractive – I certainly never lacked for male attention...not that I either looked for, nor wanted it. Shrugging, I quickly rubbed an intensive moisturising cream into face, neck and décolletage.

Unwrapping the towel, I hung it on a hook to dry out and headed back into the main cabin in search of food. The warmth of the living space felt delicious against my skin and I smiled, a genuine smile of appreciation for the pleasure it gave me. "It's the little things!" I laughed to myself, whilst placing a dish containing a ready ration into the small microwave built into the wall of the cabin.

A few minutes later I sat cross-legged on the wide bench seat which doubled as my bed, spooning up mouthfuls of my meal whilst reviewing some data on my tablet. The food was barely tolerable, consisting as it did of an artificially created protein with all the other nutrients required to enable a human to function at optimum efficiency. Any flavour seemed to have been added as an after-thought, rather than trying to create something enjoyable. I didn't mind though, it kept me fuelled up, and anyway, I had a secret stash of chocolate I'd managed to find room for in my baggage on the journey from home. By only eating a couple of squares at a time, and only after a 'meal', I had managed to eke out my meagre supply for several months.

I chucked the empty container into the trash compactor and selected an instant latte from the drink selection – that, and my two squares of chocolate were my treat at the end of the day whilst I watched an episode or two of 'Friends', an old TV series from the home planet which made me laugh.

The twin crescents of moon were high in the sky before I extinguished the lights in the cabin and pulled the heavy quilt over me preparing for sleep. Warm as the cabin currently was, I knew the temperature would soon drop and experience had shown me that it was better to be covered up before that happened.

I'm not sure how long I had been asleep before a loud alert from the onboard comms woke me with a start...I'd been dreaming of home, running barefoot through the meadow at the rear of my parent's house.

'Burrrr. Burr. Burr', the alarm sounded again. Stumbling groggily from my warm little nest I made my way the couple of steps to the control panel and activated the comms speakers.

"May Day. May Day," I heard. "Is there anyone nearby? Assistance needed. Assistance needed."

The voice was panicked and sounded out of breath.

Shivering with cold and wishing I'd wrapped the quilt round me I replied, "This is survey mission 4,

I'm in Delta quadrant. What is your position?"

"Also Delta," the voice replied. I could hear the gasps for air, whoever this person was they were heavily exerting themselves...perhaps running.

"OK. I'm going to turn on my sand crawlers' lights...tell me if you can see them." I flicked the external lights on.

"No. Oh, wait, maybe. Flash them, let me check." Dutifully I flashed the lights on and off several times.

"YES! I see you...heading your way now. I'm perhaps 3 or 4 clicks away."

I wished I could offer to head towards them but there was no way I was able to ascertain what direction to go. Normal exploration teams wore trackers for precisely these kinds of occasions, however I'd turned the locator with the comms and nothing was showing up.

"Where's your tracker? Turn it on for me and I'll come and find you." I was pulling on my work gear as I spoke – naked was good when by myself, not so good for mounting a rescue mission!

"Lost!" the voice panted. "Along with everything

else." Much as I wanted to ask what had happened, I was aware that the other person was running and needed to save their breath. I left the comms channel open though and could hear the ragged breathing; occasionally I gave a little rallying pep talk but really I could do nothing.

After several minutes I saw I tiny flickering light away to the right of my sand crawler. "Are you wearing a head torch?" I asked.

"Yup!"

"OK, I see you then. I'll head towards you." The sand crawler was already fired up. I moved slowly forwards, turning in the direction of the tiny light. Although the crawlers had a pretty good top speed I was loathe to engage it – the last thing we needed was for me to run into the person I was supposed to be rescuing. As I got closer I turned the crawler's front lights on full…

"Oh mother fucking hell!" I swore loudly. I could now see the running figure and behind them was one of the biggest tridecca beasts I had ever seen. "You better just keep running. as far and as fast as you can," I told the distant figure. "I'm upping my speed now I've seen what's behind you!" I floored the crawler and watched terrified as the creature appeared to be gaining on the running figure. I could hear the ragged breathing turn into gasps as they struggled to take on enough oxygen, clearly they were tiring – I just had to risk it and turn the speed up another notch.

Only once had I seen what a tridecca could do to a human – it wasn't a pretty sight; their triple rows of teeth could tear through the thickest work gear and they could bite a human body in half in one go.

At last I was close enough to see the face of the runner – it was a bloody mess and they were holding one arm tight against their chest. I spun the crawler round so the door was facing them... "I'm going to open my rear door," I told them. "Jump on, shut it and we'll get the feck out of here!"

I opened the door, he was very close, terror and exhaustion were writ clearly across his face. He was someone I knew only vaguely, a name, Terry, popped into my head. The tridecca was gaining, I could see the red of its three eyes and even smell the foetid breath. "COME ON!" I shouted..."COME ON!"

Terry was no more than 10 metres away from safety when the tridecca caught up with him. Its massive jaws clamped around his midsection and with a crunch his head and torso were separated from his legs which, bizarrely, hideously, appeared to keep running for a split second.

Horrified I slammed my door shut, returned to the driver's section of the cabin and sped away as quickly as I could. Terry was (had been, I corrected myself) a relative newbie to Reda, the planet we were exploring; he would have been warned about the dangers of being out of his sand crawler after dark but a warning without context can be easy to ignore. If you had never seen a tridecca, or one of the many other flesh eaters that emerged after sundown, then you may not believe the damage they do.

Having finally reached my original location, I shut down my engines, then prepared and sent a brief report to command about the loss of Terry (his surname eluded me). Sun up was still several hours away and so I undressed and crawled back into my cosy bed, still time to catch some sleep.

Terry was not the first newbie to fall foul of Reda's animal life, he doubtless wouldn't be the last and I couldn't, wouldn't lose any sleep over him. You may find that heartless and maybe it is, but I am a realist and my job has to go on...

11 May from a prompt "is that it?"

The Winning Game

'Is that it?' she asked herself as she slowly closed the door. ' Is that it?'

The build-up to this moment had been intense and had gone on for weeks...if she were being truly honest with herself, actually it had been eighteen months. Eighteen months of wondering if she could do it, or if she should do it at all. Eighteen months of deliberation, self-doubt and worry had all come down to those past five minutes.

Tilly sighed inwardly, she had often been accused of being an overthinker and a procrastinator, and she was aware that spontaneity was not one of her strong points; this would seem to be yet another one of those occasions when she could have acted much, much sooner and been better off as a consequence.

Still, no point crying about the time she'd lost when there was so much to move forward with now. She set her shoulders in what she thought must be a determined and business-like way and headed back to her corner of the open plan office. Colleagues nodded as she passed, a couple even said "hi" and she responded in kind, grateful to finally get back to her desk.

Once there, Tilly extracted a flat pack box, one of those origami-like ones that popped easily into shape and began to methodically pack it with the items both on and in her desk. It didn't take long, she was not one to keep hold of much extraneous 'stuff', and she was done within a few minutes.

She noticed a frisson of interest ripple around the office as she was completing the task; could hear a few muted comments wondering what she was up to, had she been sacked etc., etc., but decided that if no one asked her directly she would say nothing. It was none of their business after all. That thought made her smile to herself – it WAS none of their business, if they wanted to find out they would just have to wait and see!

Head held high, she marched back through the office, declining to answer any of the questions directed her way.

"Snobby cow, " she heard one of the younger women say.

'Screw you', Tilly said in her head and carried on walking…this felt GOOD.

Working in the publishing house had been a dream come true for her when she had started there almost three years ago. On paper it had seemed like the perfect job, reasonable prospects, exposure to the industry and a chance to learn how to structure her own work for submission. The reality had been rather different; far from having any engagement with authors and any hint of creativity, she was allocated mind-numbingly mundane tasks – opening the post; stapling loose items; filing; uploading things to the company's cloud storage…all things a junior would be expected to do, and for the first six months she had willingly done all those tasks. However, when things had shown no sign of changing, she was *still* being given only the menial tasks even after someone younger and less qualified joined the team, Tilly saw red and complained to her line manager.

That encounter had gone down like a lead balloon and she had begun to realise that, in all probability, she would never move up that particular career ladder. It was obvious that 'her face didn't fit', she rarely socialised out of hours, preferring to head straight home and pursue her own creative endeavours and what's more, she discovered her line manager was considerably *less* qualified than she was and therefore was probably worried that Tilly was gunning for her job. It wasn't true, she had no aspiration or desire to manage a team of people...the only characters she liked to look after were those she wrote about.

The encounter with that manager had spurred Tilly into concentrating even more determinedly on the novel she was writing. Every day she worked the meaningless tasks she was allocated and every night she went home and wrote a further 1000 words. After a year she had a sizeable manuscript, and she began to test the water by submitting a synopsis and the first three chapters to various publishers...including the one she worked for.

Several rejection letters followed, the least positive one coming from the firm who employed her...that one had hurt, particularly as it originated from her line manager, in fact she'd almost resigned at that point but had swallowed her pride – she needed the income. One letter had arrived though that expressed great interest and lots of good pointers – all of which Tilly followed and a few months, and a revised submission later, she had been offered a small book deal which she accepted.

Now at that point, she should have bitten the bullet, walked into her manager's office and tendered her resignation, but she ummed and ahhed and never actually got around to it. Consequently, it took her far longer than it should have to finish the novel and then go through all the edits, and changes deemed necessary before final publication. But she'd done it and now the book was about to be published – her editor and the publishing company had arranged a small book launch and there was to be a newspaper and TV advertising campaign...they were tipping her novel to the 'the next big thing'!

Given the publicity about to surround her they had insisted that continuing to work in a rival publishing company was no longer tenable…and she agreed – whole heartedly. She'd headed to work this morning dreading the confrontation but also relieved that the decision had been taken away from her personally. The letter of resignation was in her hand when she'd knocked on Erin Mather's door earlier.

In it, she had offered to work her full notice if required. It looked like Erin had been going to be snotty and insist she did, but she'd consulted with the head of the company over the phone whilst Tilly waited. Erin had read the full letter out, stumbling slightly when she got to the part about 'being offered a book deal by Bloomsbury', then she'd fallen silent for a few moments as she listened to the response, her face paling apart from matching red blotches on each cheek.

The phone was carefully replaced, and Erin had simply said, "You may go at once. Clear your desk."

Having expected more of a fight, Tilly was rather disappointed, but she was laughing internally at her former manager's obvious discombobulation. Doubtless if (no WHEN she self-corrected) her novel was a success, Erin would have a great deal more to explain to the head of the company.

Tilly had reached the lobby by now and she paused to hand in her key fob and name badge. The receptionist had always been pleasant to her and so she extracted an advanced copy of her book from her bag and scribbled a few words on the inside cover before handing it over saying, 'I hope you enjoy this, feel free to hand it around'.

 The receptionist congratulated her, eyes opening wide as she read the inscription 'To all my former colleagues, especially Erin Mather without whom this novel would never have been picked up by Bloomsbury's, enjoy this book and remember there are other publishing companies out there'.

As Tilly swept out of the door she could hear the receptionist chuckling and she knew by day's end there was no one in the building that wouldn't know Erin Mather's had turned down a book that Bloomsbury's had actually published.

Game. Set. Match!

12 May – reversing memories, rewinding to better days, younger times, naive principles

<u>Spin Back</u>

The record rotated, each spin reversing memories, rewinding to better days, younger times, naive principles. Morwenna gazed at the black disc on the turntable that had belonged to her 6 times great grandmother. She'd come across it by chance whilst clearing the attic in her parent's house and been intrigued enough to see if disc and player still worked, since she estimated they must be at least 150 years old.

The sound was tinny and a little faint, but she could clearly hear the lyrics..."Don't you want me, baby?"

It made her smile to think that her many times great grandmother must have listened to the tune back when she was Morwenna's age.

She kept listening, watching the disc spin round and round, her eyes began to glaze over and she felt herself becoming dizzy. The walls of her condo in the south-west of Sheffield began to melt away... 'What the fuck is happening?' was Morwenna's last thought before she toppled sidewise in a dead faint.

"Susan! Susan!" a loud voice shook her out of her faint. "Susan! Will you bloody answer me?! Your friend Sam's on the phone, wants to talk to you. Get down here!"

Morwenna opened her eyes, the pristine white of the room in her condo had been replaced with a vivid purple paintwork which was liberally covered with poor quality images of young people with bizarre hair, make up and clothes. She shut them again...tightly...then tried again – still the same. Shaking her head made no difference, other than to nearly inflict an injury as a pair of huge hoop earrings swung wildly to and fro.

"SUSAN!" the voice was much more strident now. Perhaps she was Susan? Playing along, she opened the door of the room and made her way downstairs, where an irate looking woman, wearing a hideous floral dress, stood holding out what looked like one of the telephone handsets Morwenna remembered seeing in a museum.

Bemused, she accepted the brown plastic handset puzzling at the long curly wire that attached it to a bulky looking beige-coloured base complete with dial.

"Hello?" she spoke tentatively into the mouthpiece.

"Hello you!" a female voice said back. "You took your bloody time, daydreaming again, were you? Never mind," the voice continued before Morwenna could respond. "Meet us at the bus stop at 8, Flying Alphonso Brothers are on at The Limit, it'll be a great gig. Wear that really short skirt …you look hot with that on. See ya!" The line went dead

Nonplussed, Morwenna replaced the handset back onto the rest and started to head back up the stairs.

"You and Sam going out then love?" asked a voice.

"Err, yes." Morwenna responded with no clue what

was going on but deciding it would be better to play along.

"Come and have a bite to eat then Susan. You two have a habit of getting drunk, best line your stomach!"

The woman in the floral dress was obviously Susan's mother and she served up a plateful of shepherd's pie and boiled to death carrots. Morwenna tasted the mash and meat mixture, it was delicious and she finished the entire plate, including the carrots, in no time at all. Whist she ate, 'Mum' kept up a stream of chatter in the background, various names were mentioned and Morwenna finally realised that 'Susan' was in fact her many times great grandmother – the same one who had owned the record player she had discovered.

This must be an elaborate dream she decided...but one she would really like to stay in for a while.

"It's half six love" Susan's mum said, "you know how long it takes you to get ready – best get cracking!"

Morwenna hugged her ancestor, which elicited a reciprocal hug and the comment, "Aww, you don't do that very often these days our Sue...love you lots!"

Once back in the purple hued room, she investigated the contents of the small wardrobe and found the short black skirt the girl called Sam had mentioned. Looking around for inspiration of what to wear with it, she spotted a poster on the wall – Siouxsie and the Banshees. The girl in the picture was dressed all in black and sported heavy eye makeup and wild hair...she would be the inspiration.

Dressed in a baggy black t-shirt, which slipped off one shoulder, the tight, short skirt, fishnet tights and a pair of black boots with pointy toes she found by the bed, Morwenna peered at herself (or rather her umpteenth great grandmother) in the mirror on the dressing table. She added a wide red belt that cinched in the t-shirt and found loads of plastic bangles and cheap looking necklaces – she put them ALL on.

Makeup was next – lots of it, she let her imagination go wild and indulged herself with Susan's vast array of cosmetics. The final touch was hair – a quick back comb and a liberal spray of the Insette hairspray from the dressing table was all that was required.

Morwenna smiled at the image in front of her...COOL, she thought, Grandma Susie was a looker!

The clock on the bedside table said 7.45 p.m so she scooped up a black handbag, checked for a purse with cash in it, ran down the stairs and out of the door, shouting goodbye. The bus stop wasn't far and she got there on Susan's autopilot. Waiting there was a small blonde girl wearing a strappy yellow jumpsuit. Her hair and makeup were less dramatic than the look Morwenna had gone for but nevertheless the blue mascara and fuchsia pink lipstick were striking enough.

The bus journey into the city centre felt like a history lesson to Morwenna, very little remained in 2162 of the buildings and landmarks they passed and there was quite a rundown feel to the place. Her companion chatted along as they travelled and surreptitiously passed her a small bottle full of a clear liquid...she took a swig – neat vodka! Now she understood Susan's mother's comment.

Once in the centre, they walked through an underpass which Sam referred to as 'the hole in the road', passing a large aquarium on the wall and out onto the High Street. A succession of drinks in several pubs, including one called 'The Stonehouse'

- which confusingly had a courtyard complete with a starry sky; then ensued and Morwenna felt herself getting drunker and drunker and louder and louder...it was fun!

Eventually they made their wobbly, giggly way to The Limit Club, eager to get in before the entry fee went up after 10.30pm. Sam flirted outrageously with the doorman who laughed and let them in for free.

Morwenna's 22nd century senses were assailed by a wall of noise and a unique aroma comprising of cigarette smoke, perfume, sweat, beer and weed...she recoiled a little at the sensory overload, but Sam pulled her forwards shouting over the cacophony, "Loo first!"

The ladies loo was small with a long mirror which reflected a striking persona applying a lurid shade of lipstick and wearing a long form fitting dress.

"Hey, Trev," Sam said to the vision in front of them, "how's it going?"

"Yeah, good," a surprisingly deep voice replied. "Loving this new lippy!"

Trev left the bathroom in a cloud of perfume and hairspray, making room at the mirror for the two girls to reapply lipstick and eyeliner before sharing a cubicle and having a wee – something Morwenna had already noticed appeared to be common practice.

Ablutions complete, they walked over to the bar, which was already rammed; the floor was sticky with spilt drinks and crumpled plastic glasses. Lagers in hand, the pair edged round the small dance floor, eager to see if the band were setting up but there was no sign of them, so they downed the beers and headed for a dance. "Rock the Casbah" was all Morwenna could hear but she moved to the beat.

"Now for a bit of home-grown talent that's just made it to number one on the Billboard charts," the voice of a DJ said as the song faded out…

"I was working as a waitress in a cocktail bar," sang a voice to a few jeers from the crowd.

"They were so much better before them lasses," a young man near to Morwenna said. "Remember Empire State Human? Epic bloody song, that!"

"Don't you want me, baby?" the music continued…Morwenna grew dizzy, felt like she was falling…

The sound of the intercom buzzing brought her round…"Morwenna, answer the bloody door!" said a voice.

She looked around; the bright white walls of her apartment greeted her…the dream was over, the black disc on the ancient machine was still spinning but the stylus had returned to its cradle.

13 May – prompt "I can do this"

I Can Do This!

"Okay, deep breath, I can do this." Saying the words out loud helped to calm me somewhat. I focused on the task in hand.

Three hours ago, I had been moved from the delivery ward to my own room in the maternity unit. My insides still felt as they'd been pulled out and then shoved back in again only the wrong way around, and my nether regions were sore, the stitches that had repaired the episiotomy cut pulled every time I moved.

Giving birth is not glamorous.

My newborn daughter screwed up her tiny, angry little face, ready to let loose another heart-rending scream of annoyance. Quickly pulling down my nightdress I reached into the crib and scooped her up, directing her open mouth to my nipple. That immediately had the desired result of quietening the crying. She rootled for a second or so and then abruptly latched on properly, making my eyes open wide in surprise at the strength of her suckling.

Immediately after her birth she had been placed on my chest and had found the nipple quickly enough, but her sucking had been nowhere near as vigorous as it was now.

"Ouch," I exclaimed involuntarily.

Her tiny hand gently kneaded the side of my breast and she made adorable snuffling noises as she fed. I fell in love with her all over again, marvelling at the body's ability to produce the hormones to cause such a strong and immediate bond despite the rigours of labour and delivery.

I cupped her downy head in one hand and stroked the soft cheek; becoming a mother had not been in my plans – I was supposed to be a career woman, driven, ambitious, and indeed I had done very well. Great job, big house, fancy car, travelling all over the world, I'd never felt the need for marriage and family. Finding out I was pregnant, after a brief dalliance in Paris whilst working there, had been one hell of a shock. I'd been on the pill for years, no reason to suspect it would stop working...but it had.

When I'd finally realised that I was indeed pregnant – denial can only last so long – my initial reaction was that I didn't want the baby and I set about arranging an abortion. As I wasn't sure of the dates an ultrasound scan was arranged.

Laying on the couch in the clinic, I'd feigned disinterest as the cold gel was applied to my still flat stomach and then I'd heard the sound of her heartbeat - a rapid tickerticktock – I turned my head and on the screen I could see a vaguely baby shaped 'bean'.

The technician saw my interest, "You're around 8 weeks pregnant. Baby is about 1.3 cms long. Heartbeat is healthy."

That moment changed my life, I truly hadn't believed that the embryo inside me would in any way resemble a baby so early on in pregnancy. My own heart started to beat rapidly, how could I in all conscience deny this baby a chance at life? I cancelled the planned abortion there and then and so the journey to motherhood began.

Colleagues and friends were shocked by my decision, but I was determined, and they knew that once I made up my mind, nothing would stop me. Work schedules were changed, meetings cancelled, and I personally appointed my maternity cover replacement. I read loads of books, watched numerous TV shows about pregnancy and childbirth and attended every antenatal appointment. I even took up 'pregnancy yoga' – my need to be amazing at everything I did even extended to being pregnant!

Despite all my research, when my contractions started I had a moment of mild panic and when they began to deepen I was astonished at the level of pain. My intention had been to deliver naturally with no pain relief...this lasted all of two hours before I begged for gas and air!

Baby was delivered after a 10-hour labour with me on my hands and knees grunting like a wild animal.

I wish I could say the pain stopped...but it doesn't –
it lessens, most definitely, but you still hurt!

With a satisfied 'pffff', baby stopped feeding and
my nipple popped out of her rosebud mouth. She
had a beatific look of utter contentment on her
face, which made me smile.

I carefully placed her back into the crib and took
the opportunity to grab a few minutes rest myself.
That's one thing I'd picked up at the antenatal
classes – rest when baby does.

My nap didn't last long though, I was roused by
cries from the crib...to me they didn't seem like the
same kind of wails I'd heard pre-feeding, so I
thought I'd best check for other causes – a full
nappy.

Unfortunately, that was the correct assumption.
Having never changed a nappy before I almost
considered buzzing for a midwife, but deciding I
had to start some time, I repeated my earlier
mantra, "Okay, deep breath, I can do this," and
popped the fasteners on her vest.

There was 'seepage' from around the legs of the
nappy – 'this wasn't going to be fun' I thought to
myself before peeling back the Velcro tabs.

What confronted me was utter carnage...sticky black meconium filled the nappy, spread up her back and round her front and I'd managed to smear it on the vest too. She, bless her, had stopped crying and her eyes gazed unfocusedly up at me.

By the time I'd cleaned her up I reckon I'd used a half pack of wipes and she was beginning to get grizzly again. In addition, I'd somehow wiped the tarry stuff on the side of the plastic crib and all over the mattress cover! With a degree of shame, I felt obliged to press the button to call a midwife in to help clean the crib.

She bustled in just as I'd settled baby on the other breast, she was suckling noisily, and the midwife beamed at me. "Well done! You seem to have cracked the feeding."

I grinned and indicated the crib..."Not the nappy changing though!"

"Well if it's any consolation, there's unlikely to be another one like that!" She wheeled the crib out, returning within a few minutes with a clean one.

Snuggling with my lovely daughter after she was replete, I reflected on my changed life...I could handle a rebellious boardroom more effectively than a full nappy. But I'd had to learn the skills to do so and I could learn how to be a mum too...

"Okay, deep breath, I can do this! Motherhood starts now."

14 May – prompt "starry, starry night"

Starry, Starry Night

"Starry, starry night." I hummed the tune to myself; my knowledge of the lyrics being limited to those two words. The song had only popped into my head because I was laying on a blanket on a beach, gazing up at a beautiful star-filled sky.

I'd long talked about spending a night under the stars without a tent, or shelter of any kind, but The

Peak District of Derbyshire where I live doesn't really have the climate for it. An all-expenses paid trip to Malta to write about the megalithic structures that litter the island seemed like an ideal opportunity to indulge my desire...and so here I was.

The last time I'd been to Malta I'd stayed the other side of the island, just outside Sliema, in a tourist hotel...a nice enough place but lacking in character. This time I was in a beautifully converted farmhouse in a small town called Zurrieq on the south-western side of the island – a hop and a skip from the Blue Grotto and Hagar QIm, one of the sites I was to explore and write about.

Having arrived at the airport in the late afternoon, I had been picked up as arranged by Alex, the owner of the farmhouse, not something he usually did apparently but a mutual friend had recommended the property and asked Alex to look after me. Alex had chattered nonstop on the ten-minute drive from the airport and it turned out he had lots of local knowledge about the various temples and sites all over the island, he promised to provide me with some maps on which he would mark up some of the lesser-known places.

The 'farmhouse' turned out to be a beautifully

converted old stone house in the small town of Zurrieq itself, my room was huge and there was a delightfully secluded pool. It was going to be a great base for my stay...the only downside was it was inland and the nearest beaches were, an admittedly short, drive away. Fortunately, I'd sorted out a hire car which had been parked up near the farmhouse for me, Alex handed me the key and promised to return soon with the maps.

I made myself at home, unpacked and changed into shorts and a t-shirt, before making my way to the well-equipped kitchen where Alex said I could help myself to refreshments. Perked up by a coffee and some sort of pastry I'd found, I decided to explore the local area, locate the car and perhaps pick up some provisions.

Zurrieq was small and it didn't take me long to establish that there was a lovely bakery nearby, closed unfortunately, but worth remembering. A stroll past the post office and a museum eventually led me to a small but well-stocked supermarket where I was able to buy a decent bottle of wine and some bits and pieces that would suffice as a makeshift meal for the evening. I'd already decided I was going to find somewhere where I could stargaze and didn't want to bother with locating a restaurant in which to eat.

Alex was waiting for me when I returned, and we spent a while going over the maps and guidebooks he had found to help me find my way around the many ancient sites. I asked if there was a beach he'd recommend, a quiet one...Gnejna, he said immediately, circling it on one of the maps. It was about 20 mins drive away but not a difficult route – I had my stargazing beach sorted.

I ate some of the olives, cheese and cold meats I'd bought earlier, putting the rest into a plastic box I found in the kitchen and then into my rucksack with the bottle of wine. Swapping my shorts for trousers and stuffing a sweatshirt into the bag – it was still only May and it could get cooler later, especially by the sea – I scooped up a blanket from my room and headed out to my hire car, a Suzuki Jimny.

Twenty odd mins later I arrived at Gnejna, just as the sun was beginning to go down – the view took my breath away and better still, the beach itself appeared to be deserted. I parked up, gathered my belongings and strolled down to the sandy beach where I spread out the blanket and plonked myself down.

The first stars began to appear as the sun sank in a golden splendour into the sea, my eyes ached from watching the fiery orb disappear, but it was such a mesmeric sight I couldn't look away. Finally, tearing my eyes away, I delved into the rucksack and extracted the bottle of wine and a plastic cup (not classy maybe but certainly less likely to break); and pouring a generous amount, toasted the sunset and watched the stars appear.

With my rudimentary knowledge, I was able to pick out the constellations of Cassiopeia and Ursa Minor but that was about it...I didn't care, I'd come to enjoy the beauty of a night where I could stay outside and stargaze...at least for a while.

It was getting cooler, so I finished the wine I'd poured, put on the sweatshirt and lay back on the blanket, pulling half of it over me. THIS was what I'd dreamed of for so many years – being alone outside, looking up at the night sky. It truly was more than I could have imagined, no light pollution or clouds to obscure the view.

As I watched the stars pass across the sky, it seemed that their beams of light were pinning me to the blanket; passing through my body, through the sand and rock beneath me, to emerge on the other side of the planet before looping back round to the point of origin. There was no beginning, no end, no 'me'; I was simply a part of the spiral of life, of the universe itself.

My mind drifted to all the people, the men and women of this island, who many thousands of years ago had dared to build the massive stone structures which endured to this day. What had inspired them? What had driven them? Could it have been something connected to the stars and their precession across the sky. Ancient monuments had always fascinated me, I felt connected to them in a way it is hard to communicate. I was left in awe by the scale and grandeur of them, built without any metal tools and with none of the technology we had now. Sometimes I even wondered if perhaps the old ones did have access to methods and even technology that is lost to us now...

I must have drowsed off for a while because I came to with a start and, upon checking my watch saw an hour or so had gone by. I was chilled by this point, the romance of laying on a beach in the dark seemed less appealing than a hot bath in the gorgeous bathroom back at the house. But I'd done it...I'd fulfilled a long-held dream.

"Starry, starry night," I hummed to myself.

15 May – prompt was "Once upon a time"

<u>Once Upon a Time</u>

Once upon a time; not so very long ago in the grand scheme of things; a child was born – a girl. There was, on the face of it, nothing at all special about this child or her family but, as is often the case, it is the ordinary that leads to the extraordinary.

Leah, for that was the name given to her, was a

precocious child; she was walking by eight months, talking by the age of one and taught herself to read by the age of three. Her parents were nonplussed as her older siblings had displayed none of these talents; indeed, her eldest brother was still unable to read or write as well as she, despite being five years older.

The girl was blessed with a sunny disposition and could see a positive slant to anything and everything. This made her many friends outside of the family unit but caused tension and jealousies within as her brothers and sisters saw how well loved she was by so many. They tormented and picked on her unmercifully, but she shrugged off their behaviour and simply carried on being happy...which of course annoyed them even further.

When Leah started school, she astounded her teachers by how quickly she absorbed knowledge, she was like a sponge and only ever needed to be shown something once. She learned so quickly that she was soon far ahead of the others in her class and was moved up a year and then another and another...no one knew how to deal with a child so blessed with intelligence. She could have become bored, disruptive, a problem, but Leah just kept smiling, kept being happy and kept on learning. When the schools and the teachers could no longer help her, she turned to libraries and read all she could.

To the irritation of her older sisters, Leah also grew into a great beauty; she was possessed of silver hair and deep brown eyes, a striking combination that was shared by no one in her family. She could also play any musical instrument she picked up and sing like an angel. In days of old she would probably have been called a faery child, but these were more enlightened times.

When the time came for Leah to make her way into the wider world by attending a university, her siblings were united in wishing she would go as far away as possible and never come back. With her around nothing they ever did would be good enough, for they could never hope to compete with her abilities.

Leah didn't know what to study, she wanted to learn everything and couldn't understand why she had to focus on only one area. To her mind, medicine, science, the stars, language, the way the very world works, were all connected...to study just one aspect of the whole made no sense to her at all.

She attended numerous interviews at top universities, all keen to offer her a place but none suited her – none of them was open minded enough to tailor something for her...she had to fit the mould of one size fits all. But she'd already spent too much time trying to fit in, dumbing down her abilities and dimming her light – she'd simply had enough of trying to be 'normal', she wanted to be herself. For the first time ever, Leah lost her sparkle, her joie de vie, she felt her future was being constricted by 'the muggles'; a name for ordinary people that she'd read in a book. She knew she had so much to give, if only there was a way.

At the depth of her sadness she received a strange message. "Leah, your light should never be dimmed. Call this number for a solution to your problems." Initially she brushed it off, ignored the text – the world was full of cranks and spam; but curiosity ate away at her and she called the number.

"Finally," said a male voice. "We were beginning to think you weren't who we think you are Leah."

She nearly hung up, but she was intrigued. "Who do you think I am?"

"Why, one of us of course," came the reply. "But if you want to know more you will have to meet us...what have you got to lose?"

The voice was right, what did she have to lose? And so, the next day saw Leah boarding a train to a town she'd never heard of before, from there she was to be collected and taken to meet 'the others like her'. The journey was long, and she was nervous, yet a voice inside her was telling everything was going to be alright, that she was on her way to meet the start of her destiny.

After what seemed many hours, Leah eventually arrived at what was obviously the final destination, a large gothic mansion in its own grounds. She was ushered into a lounge furnished with comfortable chairs and sofas. The middle-aged man who had, as promised, collected her from the station, patted her on the arm and said to help herself to a drink and that 'the others' would be along in a moment. She was halfway down a rather lovely cup of tea when the door swung open...

Twenty or so individuals, both male and female, entered the room; Leah stared, she couldn't help it, because each of them had silver hair and deep brown eyes...Just. Like. Her.

One of the group laughed at her opened-mouthed expression and she blushed.

"Don't worry, we all had the same reaction when we first saw each other – it's like looking in the mirror, isn't it?"

Leah nodded, dumbfounded. These people, all roughly her age, looked more like her than any of her siblings – or indeed her parents. How could this be?

Over the course of the next few hours, she learned that she was an advanced type of human, that many more like her, like them, would eventually be born. That she was a 'way shower' and a beacon for those to come...as were the others in the room with her.

The group had come together to create their own place of learning – one where the 'students' studied whatever took their fancy – no fixed curricula, or exams, just a thirst for knowledge. The aim was to continue to grow by reaching out to the others like them and in order to facilitate this they had 'spies', for want of a better name, in all the most respected universities in the UK and around the world. People like them were easy enough to spot, after all.

Leah asked how why they all looked so similar but none of the others knew for sure…it was genetic, that much they knew (and was obvious) but they couldn't yet explain why or how the genetic code was being promulgated throughout the globe. It was something they planned to explore once they had the capacity to do so.

The final question to Leah was, "Would you like to join us?"

She smiled, feeling completely at ease for the first time in her life… "Of course," was all she said.

Leah left her family and moved to the mansion within a few weeks…her siblings were relieved; she was excited, this felt like the true beginning to her life – a life far more extraordinary than could ever have been predicted when she was born.

16 May – inspired by a video of a black cat!

The Cat That Got All the Cream

There it was again! The large black cat with the aquamarine eyes I kept seeing prowling around the neighbourhood at dusk. She, for I'm sure this was a 'she cat', would make a stately procession around the duck pond before taking up a spot directly across from my window. Once there she would proceed to groom herself thoroughly, whilst all the while, at least it seemed that way to me, watching me watch her. Ablutions completed, she would saunter off, casting an over the shoulder glance my way.

I never saw the cat during the day and none of my neighbours had ever seen her – I think they thought me a little odd to be honest...a single man with a cat obsession!

The ritual of watching the cat continued for several weeks, I never tired of watching the sinuous creature I mentally christened Bast, after the Egyptian goddess. It was strangely relaxing, almost hypnotic, watching the beautiful creature stretch out an elegant leg to groom with her rough pink tongue.

One day, pre-empting her arrival, I crossed over to her usual spot on the village green and left a small saucer of double cream. Back in my cottage, I took my place beside the window and waited for her to arrive...moments later she did. Her curiosity was obviously piqued by the intruding object on the grass, but she proceeded on her usual stroll around the pond before returning to the saucer.

'Bast' sniffed cautiously at the contents of the

saucer, then dabbed one paw gently into the cream and lifted the paw to her mouth. Her pink tongue tasted the cream and, finding it very much to her taste, she licked the paw clean and bent her face over the saucer. I could almost hear the purr of satisfaction as she lapped daintily away until the saucer was clean. The usual cleaning ritual followed, and then she rose to all fours and stretched in the luxuriant way cats do. I swear she nodded her head to me in thanks for her creamy treat.

I continued to put cream out for her every day for the next week, each evening she would lick the saucer clean and appear to thank me with a dip of the head in my direction before she slunk away into the deepening night. Then on day eight she didn't show up, nor on the following two nights – I was distraught imagining the worst, perhaps she'd been knocked over, was lying bleeding somewhere – or even dead.

My anguish was real, very real, so when the following night she reappeared I couldn't resist actually going over to the green to see if she would let me stroke her. I sat near to the saucer of cream, initially I was viewed with some suspicion, but the lure of the cream was too strong to resist and Bast carefully tiptoed around me, avoiding contact. I watched her drink, little pink tongue flicking in and out of her mouth, until the saucer was clean. With a wipe of one paw she cleaned the droplets adhering to her whiskers, watching me as she did so. Emboldened by the fact that she hadn't run away I extended one hand, not expecting anything but, to my surprise she walked over to me, tail erect, and pushed her head against my outstretched hand.

For a few glorious minutes she let me stroke her head and along her back; her jet black fur was silken smooth under my hand and her purr was a deep resonant rumble which I could feel deep inside. When she'd had enough of my ministrations she simply turned and walked away, but not before she'd given me an apprising look with her aquamarine eyes.

I slept well that night, feeling that at last I had made a connection with the beautiful animal. I dreamed that Bast had moved into the cottage with me and taken up ownership of my sofa as her bed. When I woke up, I even began to look online for cat-flaps which would allow her easy access to my cottage. I stopped myself from actually purchasing one and laughed inwardly – I'd obviously been alone for far too long!

Bast and I continued the ritual of me providing a saucer of cream in return for her graciously allowing me to stroke her for a few minutes. My neighbours must have thought I'd completely lost it, sitting out on the village green in the near dark night after night, but it made me happy. That brief daily connection with the cat helped end the loneliness I'd felt since the death of my wife two years previously.

As the nights began to draw in and the temperature dropped, I had high hopes that Bast would finally decide a lovely warm indoor space would suit her...instead she disappeared. I mourned her loss and our daily interactions but decided she must already have a home somewhere else and that I had been a mere dalliance over the summer months.

One bitterly cold day in December there was a knock on my front door, a rare occurrence if I'm honest – I'd almost become a recluse when my wife had passed. I opened it to find an attractive dark-haired woman, hand raised in mid-air ready to knock again.

"Oh!" she exclaimed, flustered. "I'm sorry to

disturb you, I was passing through the village and for some reason I had an urge to see who lived in this cottage now. It was my grandmother's before she died and I always loved to visit..." her voice trailed off.

I smiled, she was clearly embarrassed, probably hadn't expected to find anyone in at this time on a Monday.

"I love it here, please – come in, have a look what I've done with the place." The truth was that I actually hadn't done very much when I moved in, almost immediately after my wife had passed away, the cottage suited me just as it was, and aside from a little painting I'd changed nothing.

"Megan," said the woman thrusting out her hand, I shook it.

"Mark," I replied, standing to one side to allow her in.

She looked around the single large room, a combined kitchen/living space with a large wood burner which was pumping out heat. "You've not changed a thing," she laughed, "such a lovely room, I'm glad you haven't!"

I offered tea, she accepted, and we drank it sitting

around the small oak table I'd made myself. Much to my surprise we hit it off immediately and the conversation flowed easily; I told her about my wife, Liz, and she described her grandmother.

"A tad eccentric, but lovely," she said. "She always used to joke that she was a witch, she even had a beautiful black cat with the bluest eyes I've ever seen. I wonder what happened to her, she disappeared when Granny died. Bast, she named her, after the Egyptian goddess."

I paled. "There was a black cat on the green over the summer, I grew quite fond of her actually and believe it or not – I called her Bast!"

Megan began to giggle. "I feel Granny's influence here! I haven't driven through this village since she died but I felt a real pull today. She was always trying to match-make for me, she insisted on meeting anyone I dated so that Bast could check them out. None of them ever met with the cat's approval! In fact, I don't think any of them were able to get anywhere near her!"

This time I laughed, "Well this Bast grew used to me and even let me sit and stroke her. Perhaps your granny would approve of me?"

We continued to chat, a definite warmth that wasn't just the heat from the log burner began to spread through me...Bast may have disappeared but it looked like she'd brought Megan to my door instead.

17 May – a rehash of a story I wrote age 15

Evolution

The cat crept through the dense undergrowth; belly close to the ground, it stalked its prey. The animal in front of the cat suddenly realised it was being pursued and began to scamper away. The cat raised up onto its hind legs, reaching half the height of a full-grown man; the front paws pointed almost carelessly towards the escaping animal and unfathomable green eyes began to glow and pulse with a strange luminescence.

The prey, a full-grown rabbit, suddenly stopped in its tracks, appeared to lift from the ground and hover. The cat's eyes were glowing like twin emeralds and an almost invisible beam of light appeared to emanate from the raised paws, ending at the rabbit suspended in mid-air. With a visible effort the cat drew the prey towards her until it was in reaching distance when she, almost lazily, batted one paw against the creature, sinking her deep claws into its flesh and pulling it to her mouth.

With a crunch she bit into the rabbit's neck, sharp teeth severing the windpipe instantly. The cat sank gracefully back onto all fours, the strange green glow fading from her eyes. Delicately the cat devoured the rabbit until all that remained was a tangle of fur and the skull.

Appetite satisfied, the large black cat set about thoroughly cleaning herself; sharp claws now safely sheathed, the rough pink tongue sloughed away the remnants of blood and flesh from the paws before using them to clean her muzzle and long whiskers. Clean and replete, the cat stretched before curling up for a well-deserved sleep.

Several hours later the cat awoke and stretched once more, she began to walk out of the woodland undergrowth towards open fields. Her body moved in a graceful sinuous fashion, muscles rippling under the sleek black fur. As she reached the very edge of the field a child's voice rang out,

"Daddy! Look at the beautiful cat! Can I have it? Please! Let me take it home!"

"I shall have to see if I can catch it first love, it may not want to be a pet."

The father and child slowly approached the cat, who stopped in her tracks and waited until they were only about 20 metres away before raising onto her hind legs.

"What's it doing Dad?"

"I don't know, love, but it's not running away so perhaps it's quite tame."

The cat's eyes began to glow the strange emerald colour again but this time, mingled with the green, was the hint of another colour, not one that could be identified, perhaps even one from an entirely new spectrum. A beam of pure concentrated energy passed from the cat to the two humans.

The child began to wail plaintively, "Daddy my head hurts! It feels like it's going to burst."

The man felt his vision beginning to blur and his head pounded with the worst headache he had ever experienced. Through his own pain he tried to comfort his child who, by now, was on his knees, sobbing and holding his head in his hands.

The beam of energy connecting cat to humans grew brighter, more intense – almost more solid. The man too fell to the ground. Indescribable pain filled his head, his brain felt as though it had grown too big to remain in his cranium. The child on the ground next to him screamed, a high, thin noise. He reached for his son's hand and held it tightly.

Through a red mist of intense pain, it seemed to the man that the cat had grown immensely in stature and now towered above them. Conscious thought became too much for him, he lay on the ground and began to convulse, shaking and shuddering. Deep red blood had begun to seep from his child's eyes, ears, nose and mouth – shockingly vivid against the pale skin. A last violent jolt of pain went through each of them...

Brains grown too large for the bone encasing them exploded outwards, bits of bone and brain and flesh flew out and away. Features dissolved and disappeared, a bloody eyeball landed at the cat's feet, she regarded it distastefully then turned away from the shattered bodies to face another large cat who had appeared from the edge of the wood.

Green eyes met green eyes and thoughts were exchanged. The female cat re-joined her mate and together they padded back to the comfortable den they had created where eight kittens waited for her to feed them. Each of the eight healthy kits shared their parents' abilities – the stage was set for a magnificent future for this new species of feline.

18 May – no prompt

Time for Tea

Emily and I first met as nervous and uncertain first year students at Sheffield University; she was studying History and I English, we were roommates in the hall of residence and quickly became firm friends.

Our friendship lasted through shared houses, graduation, raucous holidays and many, many drunken nights. It survived relationship breakdowns, marriage, children and divorce (both of us). For 42 years we shared everything that life threw at us and emerged, if not unscathed, then at least unbowed.

We didn't survive the last battle though...

At the age of 60, Emily was diagnosed with cancer – pancreatic cancer. I'd like to say she fought it bravely, but the truth was that from diagnosis to death was a mere 4 months. She, her children and I had barely come to terms with her illness before she took her last breath. My oldest, dearest friend; the one person on the planet who knew me as well, if not better than I knew myself, had been taken from my life.

I drifted through the first few weeks after her death, I missed our daily chats and the cups of tea and slices of cake which more often than not accompanied them. It had all happened so very quickly that my mind refused to catch up with reality and I kept expecting to open the front door and find her standing there. I'd see glimpses of her when I was out, the unruly mop of curly hair, which had gone grey in her early 50s and which she refused to colour. The rather eclectic outfits in the vibrant colours she had so adored. The silvery tinkle of her numerous bangles as she lifted a cup of tea to her lips.

I'm not ashamed to say I was lost without her.

Emily's eldest daughter, named Amanda after me, turned up at my door three weeks after her mum had passed away. She held a letter in her hand, addressed to me, in her mother's handwriting.

"I can't stop," she said, "but I thought you should have this, I found it in Mum's handbag when I was going through her stuff last night," her eyes filled with tears as she spoke.

Emily had been a fantastic mum and was very close to all of her four children, but there was a special bond with Amanda, her only daughter. I gave her a huge hug which made both of us cry – it seemed there was no end to the tears one could shed over the loss of someone so dear.

The letter proved to be short and to the point, not unlike Emily herself.

'My dearest friend,

As you are reading this letter it means this horrid disease has done for me and I've buggered off to heaven – or wherever it is we're supposed to go...if indeed we go anywhere.

Do me a favour and don't be too sad, I've no regrets about anything in my life and neither should you. Remember how much fun we had.

Now, do you remember how I always said I'd haunt you if I went first? Well I meant it, so, every second month, on the anniversary of whatever date I shuffled off this mortal coil I want you to set your table – tea for two – and I'll come and say hello.

I love you, old friend...

See you soon.

Emily xxx'

There was no date on the handwritten missive, but it was clearly written when she was already quite ill as the handwriting was not as flamboyant as Emily's usual style; it wavered a little in places.

I felt a tear slide down my face, but the tone and the brevity of the letter was so very Emily that I actually felt my mood lighten a little. She **had** always promised to haunt me and I had no doubt that if such things existed, if it were possible to visit someone as a ghost, then Emily would manage to do it!

My life proceeded at its normal steady pace; I continued to write, working on another novel and did the normal everyday stuff. There was a great big Emily-shaped hole in my life, but I kept busy and learned to cope.

The day which marked two months since her passing arrived. I took out the letter she had written me and; feeling a bit silly; set my dining room table with a pretty cloth, matching china and a plate of cupcakes – Emily's favourite. Since she had specified no time for her 'haunting' I decided to have everything ready at around the time she and I would often convene for tea and cakes...2.30 in the afternoon. A time we had arrived at after convincing ourselves that it was far enough away from our evening mealtime to be acceptable to eat large quantities of cake!

Precisely at 2.35pm I poured myself a cup of Assam tea, added milk and helped myself to a salted caramel cupcake from the plate. I felt a breath of air pass me...the kind of gentle breeze you welcome on a summer's day.

"Emily?"

Silence.

I took a bite of the cupcake, too large a bite, and gooey caramel dribbled down my chin.

"Bollocks!" I exclaimed.

A peel of laughter rang out from across the table – Emily's laughter!

"You always were a messy eater Amanda!" A disembodied voice spoke out. "What flavour is it? They look lush, I wish I could eat one."

Temporarily, and unusually lost for words, I simply stared in the direction of the voice. Was I imagining it, or was there really the vague impression of a human form there? I peered more closely – there was definitely something there, rather amorphous, and not really identifiable.

"Em...is that really you?"

"Well of course it is, you daft mare, who else would bother to come and haunt you?" Laughter rang out again. "Can't you see me?"

"Well no – not really – just a shimmery blob is all I can see."

"Hrrmmph. That's a bit rude! How about now?"

There was a kind of wavering in the air in front of

me and the blob began to coalesce into a form which was absolutely recognisable as my dear friend – albeit transparent and looking considerable better than when I had last seen her the day before she died.

"Wow! You did it Em, I should have guessed you'd manage it. Once you make your mind up you'll bloody find a way!"

Emily smiled smugly at me. "Surely you never doubted me for a minute?"

I had to laugh – both at what she had said and the fact that here I was, talking to a ghost...

We met up every two months after that – always at the same time. I would often question Emily on the 'after life' but she was never very forthcoming – something about there being rules on what she could say. She implored me never to share the fact that she visited me with her kids as she wanted them to be able to move on without her. I asked why she wasn't allowing me the same courtesy and her typically Emily response had been to say that I knew she never broke a promise.

Old friendships never die...they just change!

19 May – no prompt

New Age Order

Some people believe that humans have stopped evolving – that homo sapien has reached the very pinnacle of development and can go no further.

Others know that is a falsehood because they are aware that they are, if not a new race of human, then certainly the next step up the evolutionary scale. I can say this with a quiet confidence because I am one of those 'new humans'.

Let me tell you a little about myself and this world, I was born in 2235 in a small town in what used to be called the United Kingdom. Countries, borders and other such man-made constructs had ceased to become relevant after the war which had obliterated much of the global population in the 21st century. The rebuilding of society had taken a century or more and my forebears had rightly chosen to start anew, to disregard the old ways and to look at clean energies and small communities rather than attempt to repopulate old cities.

Salvaged records show us massive conurbations-London, Paris, New York, Berlin, Tokyo but we chose to complete the work the nuclear bombs had started and to raze what remained of the old-style cities to the ground. I've read that some people protested, saying that the old should be preserved, but the vast majority decided a fresh start was best course for humanity. Images of the past are preserved on the vast central database which contains all the knowledge of the past and all new and ongoing discoveries.

I grew up on a smallholding, we raised our own pigs and chickens and grew much of our own fruit and vegetables. We also had a shared interest in the local community farm, as did everyone in the locality, and from there we could obtain fresh milk and meat from the cows and sheep that roamed there. In some ways, society had reverted to the agrarian model of the distant past and yet technology was very much a part of daily life.

After the destruction of the heavy industrial past, a new wave of brilliant scientific minds began to explore ways of harnessing energy, ones which wouldn't involve burning anything, splitting the atom or extracting oil and minerals from the earth. It took until the latter part of the 22nd century but a way was discovered to capture an endless source of energy directly from the atmosphere. Because no one could claim ownership of the atmosphere, no one could attempt to monetise this energy source and so it was available for all to use at no cost.

We learned many lessons from the past as we rebuilt the future; no one is allowed to own huge amounts of wealth – in fact money no longer exists in the same way it did before – we don't need it. Everyone has access to all that they need, if someone wants more, they can have it, but in a society based on equality for all, anyone demonstrating excessive greed is easily spotted and regarded as a pariah. Of course, people still exist whose primary drive IS having more than everyone else; but when there is no competition for resources and where having more is not regarded as admirable, these creatures are few and far between.

I'm digressing though! Human evolution is where this started so let me continue.

Everyone knows that human DNA is comprised of two strands...the double helix, however, back in the 21st century before the bombs fell, 'spiritual' beliefs began to emerge based on 12 strand DNA activation. Of course it was regarded as new age nonsense by mainstream science and no research was conducted. In our more enlightened times however, scientists began to look at the possibility that 21st century beliefs actually had some basis in reality.

They discovered that 12 strand DNA was not only plausible but likely and began to experiment using sound, specifically Solfeggio frequencies as had been mooted 200 years previously, to attempt to activate the additional strands. What they found, was that in certain people, specific sound frequencies did in fact alter their DNA.

My mother and father were amongst those whose DNA was recoded to 12 strands and I, in turn, was born with 12 strand DNA. All of us with this new variant have unusual abilities, at least by '2 strand human' reckoning. Most of us are telepathic, some of us also have telekinetic abilities and we are all able to move ourselves to new locations using only the power of thought. Along with these 'psychic' gifts we are also highly intelligent as a result of being able to access more of our brain's inherent cognitive potential...we can see more possibilities than the average human and this has led to even greater advances in science and medicine.

I am one of the few '12 stranders' who, in addition to the usual enhancements, also has the ability to heal. This was something I first discovered age ten when I found one of our chickens had been badly injured by a fox; I had cradled the bird in my arms and literally wished it was healed. I imagined it whole and running around with its chicken friends and had been aware of a warmth and faint glow emanating from my hands into the bird. Within minutes it had begun to mend and by the end of the day it was running around with the rest of the hens – just as I'd wished and imagined.

My parents witnessed this early healing and

encouraged me towards medicine; they believe, as do I, that every child will exhibit a unique skill or trait which should be honed and developed – IF the child wishes to.

More and more of us are now being born with 12 strand DNA, but it seems that not everyone is able to attain this new level and that some people don't believe it is even possible. Despite concerted attempts by our scientists and by healers like me, there are some humans who seem destined to remain as '2 stranders' and this is beginning to cause some divisions in what had been a harmonious society. Our hope is that we are advanced enough to ensure that we can ride out this storm and avoid the inequalities and segregations we see happened in the past.

All things change – humanity is no different, we must learn to accept this and continue to grow and develop. The future is ours to nurture. The past is full of lessons to learn. The present is our chance to be the best we can be...

20 May from a prompt "how special am I?"

How Special am I?

I'm a dog, but not just any dog, I'm a very, very special dog – according to my pet human.

Of course I know It, but it's always nice when she tells me, and she does – often. Honestly, she tells me so often that I wonder if she thinks I have some sort of memory problems!

Take today for example, she got up early and was doing that human thing of standing in the indoor rain; she does it every day, voluntarily. I don't get it personally because I really dislike it when she insists on making me stand under the rain maker. Anyway, she was getting wet through and had that foamy stuff on her head when I heard something that I just had to bark at.

The more I barked, the more I wanted to bark – it's addictive, you know! I got so giddy that I started running around, it feels so good to do that, you humans should give it a go.

Lara, my human, banged on the see-through part of her rain box.

"Special!! Be quiet!"

You see, she just can't help herself. I tried to stop barking and dashing around, honestly I did, but I was having so much fun that I couldn't. I ran back into the room where Lara was doing the getting wet on purpose thing and ran straight into her legs, just as she was stepping out of the box.

"Special! Calm down. Stop running about!"

I was so happy she was out of the box and done getting wet on purpose and I wanted to tell her, so

I jumped up and down some more to get her attention. She did that thing she often does, shaking her head and saying something under her breath that I can't quite make out, it sounds a bit like "whatever did I do to deserve you!" and I feel proud that she feels that way about me.

Lara took her time sorting herself out after getting wet, first she rubbed herself all over with a huge towel, much bigger and softer than the one she uses on me when I've jumped in a puddle. Then she picked up something and held it under her each arm, whatever it was it made a strange hissing noise I didn't like. Finally, she put on her clothes...why do humans wear things, I wonder – perhaps you'd grow fur like me if you stopped covering up. I thought she'd finished and was getting excited, perhaps we could go for a walk, or I'd get fed, or at least some attention...but no, Lara got out the horrid noisy blowy thing and pointed it at her head! She kept pointing it at me too which I didn't like very much, it makes me want to snap and bite at the wind it makes.

After what seemed like forever, she put down the noisy thing, shook her head from side to side and said, "Not bad for and old bird eh Special?"

Bird? I looked around but couldn't see one

anywhere, sometimes Lara says the strangest things! We headed downstairs then, I was so eager to get to the bottom that I actually jumped the last 3 or 4 steps and ended up skidding on the hard floor…I kept forgetting it was slippery and not soft like the floor upstairs.

Behind me I could hear laughing and then, "You never learn do you Special? Still it must be nice to have your energy and bounce!"

Good, we were going to the kitchen, my favourite place in the whole house – well apart from my huge soft bed which I let Lara share with me. I did the little "yip" that means "I'm excited" and jumped around a little bit near my food bowl; I wish humans understood doggy language better…doesn't she know that means feed me? It doesn't mean fill up the shiny thing with water and get one of your cups out of a cupboard.

I yipped again…"Oh, sorry Special, are you hungry?"

I span around a couple of times…yes, yes, yes! Lara picked up my bowl and opened another cupboard – the one where I knew MY food was kept. Hurry up, hurry up! Whining a bit, I was sooo hungry, I licked my chops as the bowl was placed in front of me. At last!

My muzzle was in that bowl and I was snorting up the delicious food before Lara had even stood up. I love food and I love eating. After sleeping, and barking, oh – and running, food is my favourite thing.

Face buried in my bowl, I still heard the door to the outside being opened. GARDEN! I couldn't decide, food, garden: garden, food? When I heard the sound of Lara, MY human, talking to the uppity cat from next door, my mind was made up...garden. I took a last big mouthful of food and ran as fast as I could on the slippery floor; my claws make an interesting clicking sound when I run really fast.

I launched myself out of the door onto the grass...so many exciting smells and noises out here. CAT! I could see her having her belly tickled by my Lara – this was most definitely not on. Barking loudly as I ran over, the cat - cheeky supercilious beast - rolled over onto all fours and in one smooth jump landed on top of the fence, from where she eyed me carefully. It's not fair...why can I never catch her? Still, I could bark, and I knew she couldn't, so I decided to show off a bit and put on a really good bark show.

"SPECIAL!" hollered Lara, "for the love of God, put a sock in it. Why must you make that noise every single time you see a cat?"

Sock? Now I was confused, where's the sock? I like socks, especially the ones on Lara's feet. I ran around a bit...no socks out here. I could see Lara watching me, shaking her head and smiling, I think that means she loves me!

"Come on pooch, time for a walk." Who is pooch, I thought for a second before zoning in on the word 'walk'...YAY!

Lara clipped my lead onto my collar, I don't like the lead but I know it keeps me safe because I often get so excited that I don't look where I'm going. I once ran onto a road and nearly got squashed by a car...well at least that's what Lara said once she caught me.

We went down to the stream, I like it down there and I like getting wet there – much better than the indoor rain – and there's lots of interesting smells too.

There was another dog down there with his human. I like it when that happens because usually me and the other dog can have lots of fun chasing each other whilst the humans talk. I was having a lovely time Lara kept shouting at me to be careful as the other dog was just a puppy...err, excuse me – I think I worked that out!

Best day ever! Food. Cat. Walk. Another dog...happy Special!

*

On the bank of the stream, Lara was chatting to the other person as they watched the dogs play.

"If you don't mind me asking, why is your dog called 'Special'?"

Lara laughed, "I know, it's a stupid name, isn't it? I adopted him from a rescue centre when he was still quite young. The staff had named him Cecil and I decided I liked the name, so it stuck BUT my granddaughter was only small when I got him, and she lisped quite badly. Whenever she tried to say Cecil, it came out as 'Thetthil' which sounded a lot like the way she said 'special' and so Cecil became Special and has lived up to that moniker everyday since!"

21 May – no prompt

Blood Ties

As she wiped the dust from the top of the old roll top desk, Rachel recalled how much she had loved this particular piece of furniture as a child. It broke her heart to see how unloved this, and all the other beautiful items in the house, were now. Until a will was found, the house and all the contents were settling into silent decrepitude.

After carefully dusting all the other furniture, giving the curtains a good shake and running the vac over the faded carpet she found herself drawn back to the old desk. She seated herself on the dining room chair which had always been used by anyone working at the desk, and slowly, almost reverently rolled up the cover to reveal the fascinating interior.

As a child, Rachel had been allowed to play at the desk; the myriad small drawers with the space on the front for a label and racks for letters and other oddments had fascinated her. Looking at it now with the eyes of an adult, she was still beguiled by the romance of the piece of furniture; she imagined sitting there herself wearing a long gown, writing letters using pen and ink.

Smiling, she noticed that a couple of the brass label holders on the front of the drawers still held pieces of paper carrying words written in her own childish hand. One read 'old love letters' and the other 'bits and bobs'. Both struck her as odd things for a young child to write, but she had spent a lot of time in this house with its elderly inhabitant so guessed she had picked up the phrases that way. On a whim she opened the drawer labelled 'bits and bobs', it was full of an odd selection of, well...bits and bobs. Rachel ferreted around; paper clips, elastic bands, some old coins and a pencil sharpener. Just as she was about to shut the drawer, her questing fingers alighted on something more interesting...a small key.

It was a pretty key, if pretty was a descriptor applied to such an object. Small, no longer than the first joint of her little finger and gunmetal grey in colour. The head of the key was in the shape of a triquetra and the shaft was rounded with only one bit, it was obviously at least as old as the desk itself, possibly older. Rachel held it in her hand, feeling strangely attached to it for some reason. She decided not to put it back in the drawer and instead dropped it into a pocket of her jeans.

Next she pulled open the drawer she had once upon a time labelled 'old love letters'. A small bundle of letters rested there, tied together with a pale purple ribbon. It seemed almost disrespectful to open and read any of them, but curiosity overwhelmed her – she couldn't remember there being any letters like this when she played at the desk as a child.

The letters, six in total, were addressed to 'Violet Jenkins, Mastin House, Eyam', the house Rachel was sitting in, and were all from a Robert Wilkinson written in a beautiful curling script. Each letter began the same way, 'My dearest Violet, my heart still sings when I think of you, my darling'. Judging by the content, Violet and Robert had obviously been very much in love and Rachel wondered why she'd never been aware of this romance before. As she reached the end of the first letter, a possible reason became clear – Robert was writing to Violet in 1917 and a town called Passchendaele was mentioned.

Rachel took a shocked breath, she was a bit of a history buff and was aware that Passchendaele was the site of one of the bloodiest battles of the First World War. Reading more of the letters, which chronologically appeared to be separated by a couple of weeks, Robert wrote of the 'stinking, cloying mud' and how he hadn't felt completely dry for what felt like eternity. He told of the incessant sound of gunfire, how he couldn't hear any birds and how he longed to be back home in Eyam with 'his Violet'. Tears rolled slowly down Rachel's face, poor Robert obviously never had returned home, the last letter was dated August 1917.

She dashed the tears away with the back of one hand, feeling as if she had uncovered something

Great-Great-Aunt Violet hadn't wanted to be known. As far as she knew, her elderly relative had never spoken about a lost love and she had never married, preferring instead to live alone, a recluse who nonetheless loved her littlest great-grandniece and welcomed her with open arms and luscious homemade cakes. Rachel knew that Violet's only brother, George, had also been killed in the Great War, leaving a young wife and twin boys; one of whom was Rachel's Great-Grandfather. George would have inherited Mastin House had he survived the war, but the house had stayed with Violet after the death of her parents because his young widow had requested it. She had moved in with her own parents after the death of her husband and stood to inherit a wonderful property in nearby Grindleford. That particular house had long since been sold and Rachel had never even been there, although she had seen some old pictures.

Rachel had loved visiting Violet as a child and continued to visit regularly as she grew into adulthood. A close bond existed between them, fostered by a love of Mastin House and the pretty village of Eyam. The pair would often venture into the village, and potter around the churchyard where Violet would tell her grandniece stories of the plague and the villager's resilience in the 17th century. She'd been due to visit the day Violet had been found dead by a concerned villager, having apparently tripped and fallen down the stairs. That had been months ago now, almost a year in fact, but Rachel still visited every other week, checked for mail, dusted each room and let a little air in to the lovely old house lost in a limbo of uncertainty over its future.

Sighing and carefully re-folding the final letter before putting it back into its envelope, Rachel was just about to put the letters back into the drawer when she noticed something she'd never spotted before...the drawer seemed too short for the depth of the desk. Testing her theory, she pulled open the matching drawer on the other side of the desk; it slid out considerably further.

Intrigued, she tugged the letter drawer and removed it from the wooden runners, pulling it out completely. She felt the back of the space, tapped, it sounded hollow! Using the torch on her mobile phone, Rachel could see what appeared to be a keyhole on the right; fishing the key she'd found earlier out of her jeans pocket, she managed to fit it into the hole and turn it. It was very awkward as the space was narrow, anyone with larger hands would have found it impossible. There was a slight click and the back of the drawer opened up, revealing an envelope which she grasped and pulled out of the space.

'Last Will and Testament of Violet Jenkins' it said in an elaborate cursive script on the front of the envelope. She was stunned...somehow she had managed to find what everyone had been wondering about since Violet's untimely death!

Rachel opened it, she knew she shouldn't but couldn't resist; in addition to a legal document there was a single sheet of notepaper bearing her relatives handwriting... 'I knew you'd find it, my girl! Enjoy Mastin House, it is my last gift to you.'

22 May from prompt_"It was the smell that hit first, the memory it triggered"

Survivor

It was the smell that hit first, the memory it triggered; Helena recoiled and quickly shut the door again. She hadn't been prepared for that – for all her outward composure, she was obviously going to be much more affected by this than she had thought.

"Are you OK love?" The concerned voice of her husband, Aidan, broke through. "We don't have to do this now you know; there's no rush is there?"

She turned to him, grateful that he had insisted on coming along with her today, knowing that if he hadn't, she would already be back in the car and heading home.

"I'll be fine sweetheart, it's just such a long time since I've been here...so many memories, most of them bad ones. I hadn't expected to be so affected by it...you know me, I can cope with most things life chucks at me!"

Aidan grinned, "I know you pretend you can deal with everything Helena, I also know you well enough to understand that sometimes even you need someone to lean on!"

She stuck out her tongue but didn't disagree with him. Facing the door again, she once more turned the handle and pushed it open. There was the smell again, a combination of mustiness, disinfectant, sweat, stale cigarette smoke all overlaid with an aroma that Helena had always identified as fear. Nausea coiled in her belly and a cold sweat broke out all over her body, but she grabbed Aidan's hand and stepped into the echoey entrance hall.

"I've got to face my fears," Helena said out loud. Aidan squeezed her cold, clammy hand in reassurance, and they pushed on into the large hall with its long, cold and dead fireplace. It should have been a welcoming space, the fireplace was large and provided a good focal point, inviting people in; the sweeping wooden staircase was elegant and the stained glass in the windows either side of the large door should have dappled the room with coloured light. But the overall effect was one of perpetual neglect, of lost opportunity of an abiding melancholic darkness.

Helena shuddered in distaste, she remembered the first time she'd been brought here, aged just 13 and keen to be a part of what she considered to be the 'in crowd'. It had felt exciting, naughty, adventurous to attend a party with a bunch of other girls from her school and she'd jumped at the opportunity when asked. It had been a surprise to discover that the guest list consisted of a bunch of young girls and several older men…ranging from perhaps their late 30s to at least 70, but her school mates didn't seem to think it was anything out of the ordinary, so Helena had felt pressurised to just play along.

She'd been plied with drink and encouraged to try smoking, the mix of which had soon found her with her head down the loo violently vomiting whilst one of the men held her hair back and made soothing noises. She'd been too ill that first time to realise that he had also been stroking her small breasts. A taxi had been called for her and she'd left that first party early but the second and subsequent occasions had been very different.

It had taken several years of therapy before Helena had been able to fully remember what had been done to her in this house. At the time she had only been aware that what was happening to her was wrong, that she didn't like it, that at times it was painful but still she kept going back to those 'parties'. When finally the police had become involved, after the parents of one of the girls spotted bruising and personality changes in their daughter, a catalogue of abuse had been uncovered.

The group of girls, ranging in age from 13, Helena's age up to 18 and numbering more than 20 in total, had all been groomed. The first time they attended a party they were exposed to only alcohol and tobacco – this was the test, if the male attendees liked the girl in question they would be invited back and this time the alcohol would contain Rohypnol. Once they were in a state of stupefaction, the men would use the girls however they wished.

Helena would often wake up back in her bedroom, with no memory of how she'd got there. Her body would ache and she'd find random bruises, in the shape of fingerprints, in her most private places. Once she even thought she could see tooth marks on her inner thigh. She'd become withdrawn and her schoolwork suffered but for her at least, the ordeal had only gone on for six or so months before the police had stepped in. A couple of the older girls had been caught in the abusers' grasp for three years or more and one of them ultimately committed suicide once the full extent of the abuse she had suffered had been exposed.

Jolting herself back to the present day, Helena swallowed the bile she felt rising. "I know I can't turn back the clock, but I wish I could confront those bastards now! I'd cut their nasty little cocks off and stuff them as far down their throats as I could before stitching up their mouths and leaving them to suffocate!"

Aidan chuckled, "You have a way with words my

love and a vivid imagination, but you know you wouldn't do that! Most of the old twats are dead and buried now and those that aren't are still in prison. You are the survivor; you are the one who came out on top. It was understanding what happened to you that let you become the person you are now…remember that."

"I hope you aren't saying I should thank those dirty old gits are you?" Helena spluttered in mock indignation, knowing that he hadn't meant that. "You're right though, what happened did ultimately make me a force to be reckoned with."

She walked around the hall, opening the doors that led off it. "You know, when I saw this place come up at auction my first thought was revulsion that he or his family would profit from someone innocently buying it without knowing its history. Then when I saw he was dead and there was no family I wondered if it could me my chance to wipe the past clean. I know it's a bit further out of town than our usual developments Aidan, but do you think we could do something with it. I got it for a song you know…turns out that too many people do know what went on here and won't touch it with a bargepole!"

"I think there's a definite potential to knock the

bloody place down and start from scratch! It's not listed and the grounds are huge. I had a word with our architect who talked to the planning dept; they've indicated that they'd look very favourably on a new development here. We could get 15 to 20 properties, perhaps even leaving the footprint of the house as an open space in the centre...a memorial garden if you like."

"Love it!! And I love you Aidan Collins. Perhaps something good can come of this place and all the dark memories. Now let's finish having a look around and then we'll arrange to meet with the architect and start making some plans!"

23 May – from a prompt It was one of those days wasn't it?

Just One of Those Days

It was one of those days wasn't it? You know, one of those days when it doesn't matter what you do because nothing will work out the way you want it to.

Kate dragged her hands through her hair for the umpteenth time in the past hour; a habit that had started in childhood and which she just couldn't shake. As a consequence, her naturally curly red hair was now sticking out around her head in a puff ball, dandelion clock kind of way.

The day had started well enough, when she'd actually got up when the alert on her phone went off, rather than turning off the alarm and going back to sleep which was her usual routine. Unfortunately, things had gone rapidly downhill after that auspicious start. Firstly, the shower had suddenly started pouring out cold water just as she'd lathered up the shampoo. No amount of fiddling with the dial had improved the temperature so she had been forced to endure an icy cold rinse.

Emerging shivering from the shower cubicle she had realised she'd forgotten to get fresh towels out of the airing cupboard on the landing. Trotting naked across the laminate floor, dripping water with every step, she retrieved a bath sheet and wrapped it around herself, before grabbing a smaller towel for her hair and heading back to the bathroom. A wet spot caused her to slip and almost do the splits, at some cost to her groin, and she swore loudly,

"Fuck, fuck, fuckity fuck!"

Hobbling and clutching the top of her left thigh, she made it back into the bathroom without further incident and managed to wrap her hair in the second towel. The radiator didn't seem to be on, and it was chilly in the small room so she dried herself as quickly as she could, before spraying anti-perspirant under her arms. It felt strangely sticky and didn't smell like her usual spray...she couldn't have, surely? Scarcely daring to, she looked more closely at the can in her hand, it was bloody hairspray!

"Christ in a handcart!! Fuck my life!"

Grabbing a sponge from the side of the bath (after first checking it wasn't the one she used to clean the loo with) Kate scrubbed her armpits viciously until she was satisfied all traces of hairspray had been removed, then dried off and tried again...this time making sure she picked up the right can. By now thoroughly chilled, she headed towards her bedroom being careful to avoid the wet patches on the landing this time. Choosing jeans and a hooded sweatshirt she dressed quickly and pulled a pair of trainers out from under the bed...her feet were too cold to continue barefoot.

The doorbell rang just as she was finishing tying the laces; it rang again and then a third time before she'd done. Cursing at the impatience of whoever was pushing the button she ran out of the bedroom, straight onto a small pool of water where she skidded almost causing her to tip down the stairs. By the time she reached the front door, whoever it was had disappeared leaving only a crumpled piece of card shoved into the letterbox…'We're sorry we missed you' it read?. 'Your parcel will be taken to our nearest depot from where you will be able to collect it in 24hrs. Alternatively please contact us to arrange for a redelivery'.

"Shit!" Kate exclaimed, the only delivery she had been expecting was a gift for her god-daughter's birthday in two days' time. She'd have no option to drive to the depot, which she knew from experience was 35 miles away, to pick up the parcel.

Well there was nothing she could do about that now; she'd just have to make the trip tomorrow afternoon if little Grace was to get her birthday present on time.

Still limping a little from the first Torvil and Dean impression of the day, Kate went to the kitchen...tea and toast would be great, she thought to herself, just what she needed to restore some calm in fact. Then she remembered that the milk had gone off and she'd run out of bread the other day. She felt her irritation increase a further notch, sod it, there was a Costa on the way to the supermarket, she'd stop for a cappuccino and a blueberry muffin.

Gathering up a few of her selection of 'bags for life' and making sure her purse was in her handbag, she headed for the door...'KEYS!' an internal voice said just in time! Of course, they weren't where they should be, and it took several minutes of swearing and trying to remember when she had last seen them before they turned up in the pocket of a coat on the coat rack. 'Try again', she thought to herself, feeling a sense of relief that she'd managed to avoid locking herself out of her own house (again!).

Costa was busy and they'd run out of blueberry muffins so she had to settle for a lemon and poppy seed one, not her favourite but beggars can't be choosers, and at least they hadn't run out of coffee! Kate began to experience a feeling of wellbeing as the sugar and caffeine hit her system;

OK, so the day hadn't begun so well but it was getting better.

Famous last words – when she returned to her car there was a small but noticeable dent in the driver's door – the kind you get when another car door has opened against it with some force. There was no car parked next to hers now, but that dent had definitely not been there when she drove into the car park...the other driver must have seen the damage and chosen to bugger off rather than explain.

"AAAAAAARRRRGGGHHHH!" it was as close to a scream as she dared, given the public location.

Fuming, she got in the car and drove to the supermarket. Not taking any chances, she parked in an absolutely empty section of the car park, which meant a bit of a walk to the store – with an aching leg. For the first time that day, Kate managed to accomplish a task with no further problems and was back home within the hour having bought everything she needed – including a card for Grace and a roll of wrapping paper with unicorns on it. The house though was freezing cold; she checked the boiler; a warning light was flashing an error code and for a change it wasn't the one saying that the water pressure was low – she knew how to fix that issue. After consulting the manual, this latest code seemed to mean a plumber was needed.

An hour later, her hair looking as if she had been dragged through a hedge backwards, Kate finally managed to speak to a plumber who said he could call round within the next 40 minutes as he was already in the neighbourhood. It had only taken 15 calls to numbers she'd found online before she'd hit upon one who could help.

She put the shopping away and found a baggy old cardigan to go over the sweatshirt, she really was chilly, the boiler must have been off for a while for the house to get so cold. The doorbell rang and this time she got to the door before the other person buggered off. A rather attractive man, about her age, with short black hair, deep brown eyes and carrying a workman's toolbox stood there.

The man's eyes widened, and Kate suddenly became aware that she probably looked like a bag lady, what with the shapeless cardigan, wild hair and makeup-free face – but she didn't care, he was here to fix the boiler, not picking her up for a date.

The plumber was called Greg, and he and Kate chatted whilst he fixed the boiler and restored heat to the house. By the time he'd done, and they'd shared a pot of tea together – with milk – they were getting on like old friends, he was even teasing her about her wild hair, and she was regaling him with the story of her day from hell.

As he left Greg lingered on the doorstep. "Err, I don't suppose you'd like to come out with me sometime, Kate? Only I've really enjoyed talking to you this afternoon."

Kate grinned…of course she would! Sometimes great things can happen on even the most calamity filled days.

24 May – no prompt

Human Being not Human Doing

 'To Do List' Emma wrote in bold capitals at the top
of a page of A4 paper. She did this every morning
and generally wrote at least 15 'to dos' on the
page. If she reached the end of the day and hadn't
put a tick against a task to indicate its completion,
she would inwardly berate herself and ensure it
was the first thing written on the following day.

To label Emma a 'bit of high achiever' would be akin to saying that the Pope is a 'bit of a Catholic'. Think of the most driven, most ambitious, hardest working person you know and then imagine that times two. The only time Emma wasn't busy with something was when she was asleep; and she only slept for five hours per night, going to bed at midnight and rising at 5 a.m every day, including weekends.

Before she sat at her desk to write out the day's tasks, Emma had already put in an hour's exercise in her home gym, meditated for 40 mins, journaled extensively and found three things to be grateful for. This morning routine, a ritual almost, had come about after she had read the advice of an American business mindset coach who claimed, 'no one could be successful without a morning routine'. She'd also had a green smoothie and numerous supplements in lieu of breakfast. At the age of 41, Emma was the Head of Corporate Law at a large international firm based in London. She had all the trappings; fancy apartment, sports car, foreign holidays; and was widely tipped to make partner status within the next few months. Tall and glamorous with a toned body, thanks to the daily work outs and constant health food kick, Emma was an outwardly very attractive, very successful woman...she was however disliked almost universally within the firm and bore the nickname 'Ice Maiden'.

If she was aware of the way people felt about her, she never let on and never appeared to let anything worry or trouble her. She treated people like cogs in the machine of business, they were useful but replaceable if they didn't fit well or perform to expectations. If someone had told her she was ruthless she would have taken it as a compliment.

On this particular day, the first thing on her list was to fire one of the interns; an older than the usual fresh out of uni graduates the firm tended to attract. This intern was on a second career, having embarked upon a law degree at the age of 35, meaning they were on the bottom rung of the career ladder aged almost 39. It made no sense to Emma, who saw life as a linear progression via a series of structured steps; the concept of changing direction, trying new things and accepting that life needn't be mapped out was a complete anathema to her. The intern, Claire, had confused Emma from the word go. Claire was relaxed and fun to be around, colleagues and clients alike got on well with her; at the regular staff socials there would always be a crowd gathered around her whilst Emma stood in imperious isolation clutching a glass of expensive mineral water.

At 8.55 a.m. Emma paid a visit to her private bathroom where she applied her trademark bright red lipstick and ensured that not one blonde hair in the immaculate 'up do' was out of place. At precisely 9 a.m she buzzed her P.A. to bring Claire into the office.

It took a few moments for the intern to arrive and Emma had allocated a maximum of 15 minutes to this first task. Smiling pleasantly, Claire accepted the seat Emma pointed out to her. She had a reasonable suspicion as to why the Head of Corporate Law had asked to see her, but she wasn't going to give the other woman any clue...let her come out with it herself, she thought, relaxing back into the chair.

"Claire, thank you for coming. I've been reviewing your progress since your internship began. Mixed, is I think the best I can say. You seem to be attracted to the cases which will yield the lowest returns and spend way too long getting to know people instead of simply completing the task in hand. Your way of working is simply not compatible with mine and I'm afraid we're going to have to let you go. Thank you for your efforts. You may go now."

Claire sat up straighter, so her suspicions had been correct.

"I may go now; I may also stay and give you a bit of advice before I go, Emma Middleton. You can listen and take action, or just ignore it and carry on the way you have been doing, your choice, but if I were you, I'd go with the first option."

For once Emma was shocked into silence, Claire ploughed on.

"You may be beautiful, you may be wealthy, you may feel you have your life all mapped out and that everything is always your way or no way. But when you go back to your fancy apartment, who do you talk to? Who holds you if you ever feel sad...do you ever feel anything, Ice Maiden? What will happen to you if this business ever merges or is taken over?

Do you think a new regime would automatically take you on; you with the reputation of being a prize bitch?

I've already lived more of a life than you; I have children, a loving partner, friends and family who I care about and who care for me. What do you have…money, looks, fancy clothes – I'd much rather be me than you! You are so one-tracked on what you perceive as success, that you have forgotten how to actually have a life, forgotten how to just BE; you feel the need to fill your emptiness by working, by having a regimented ruddy 'to do list'," Claire pointed at the neatly written list on the desk. "You know why I studied law? I used to be a counsellor, a bit new age for you I think, and time and again I came across situations where people, good people, were being screwed by multi-national corporations. I decided to learn how to fight for people by learning the legal tricks that corporates adopt. So, it's actually me who should be thanking you, Emma, I've learned your nasty little tricks and am ready to use them myself. Oh, and one last piece of advice, learn to listen to your heart, I know you still have one, only once you learn to love what's inside will you ever be able to work out who you really are."

With that parting shot, Claire got up and left the room without a backward look, leaving Emma open-mouthed in astonishment. Her initial reaction was to rage, to demand Claire be escorted from the building but what was the point, the woman was leaving anyway. If the truth be known, much of what Claire had said had really hit home. Emma realised that she had become ensnared in a trap of her own making; she spent so much time in enforced busyness that she had forgotten how to connect with herself. Every day was almost exactly like the one before, she had become so wedded to her routines and rituals because it was easier than stopping and thinking about what she really, truly wanted.

Well she was thinking now, and the sad fact was that she didn't know what she wanted. She had mapped out her life based on how she had envisaged success when she was a 15-year-old school swot. But her life was largely meaningless, she saw that now with a clarity that was both startling and upsetting...who would miss her if she were gone? The answer was no one and that was a chilling thought.

That single conversation became the turning point in Emma Middleton's life, if only she had known earlier that it was that simple. When she chose to drop out of her busy mind and into her higher heart everything changed and the corporate lawyer became an advocate for those who needed her help; the lost, the lonely, the poor, the disenfranchised.

25 May from a prompt "he watched helpless in the darkness of the cave"

Blood Eagle

He watched, helpless in the darkness of the cave, whilst outside the remnants of his village continued to burn and men, women and children ran in fear of their lives.

A tear of helpless anger slid slowly down his cheek, how had it come to this and why had he not understood the signs, which, with the benefit of hindsight, had been clear to see. He could hear people, HIS people, calling out for him.

"Prophet, where are you? Save us!"

Bunching his fists in rage, he watched as one of the invaders casually speared a fleeing woman in the back; the child she was carrying, no more than an infant, fell to the ground. Laughing, the soldier picked up the baby, threw it into the air and skewered the child on his knife as it fell earthwards.

Pressing himself back deeper into the cave, he vomited in disgust; a hot outpouring of bile in response to the carnage he had just witnessed. It was as well he had chosen to look away at that point, because what had followed as the bearded assassin had retrieved knife and spear from his victims would have doubtless resulted in him crying out and betraying his position.

The killings continued until every man, woman and child had been slaughtered. Even the goats which were kept in a fenced field during the night were despatched. The soldiers, if that's what they were, showed no mercy; on the contrary, they appeared to delight in finding ever more inventive ways to kill their unarmed and unprepared victims. It seemed to be in fact an elaborate game to them. Several of the village's fittest men were left until the very last, herded together and forced to witness the unspeakable deaths of their families. Once sure no one remained alive, one of the invaders, a tall, well-built man with facial features barely visible beneath a mask of blood asked the traumatised men if they wished to join the fighters or die a painful death.

One of the men, a known and disliked troublemaker among the villagers, agreed with alacrity to joining the band of mercenaries, telling the blood-soaked inquisitor that he had no love for this village or its people. He was taken aside and marked with the sign of the new order – a square turned on one corner with each side extended downwards. The remaining villagers refused to co-operate, and each was pinned face down to the ground, arms extended, whilst rib bones were separated from spinal columns and pulled back to reveal the lungs. Still alive at this point, the men's lungs were lifted out of the chest cavity and placed on the spread apart rib cage.

The fighters whooped and cheered, drinking the village supply of ale and taking bets on which man would last the longest. Some of them retrieved the bodies of younger females and used them to satiate the blood lust further...

When the sickening revelry eventually came to an end and the last tortured man had drawn his final breath, the invading forces collapsed and slept. Back in the cave on the hillside above the village where he had hidden, the man they called prophet became aware of the relative quiet and uncurled from the foetal position he had adopted. From his spot at the very rear of the small, narrow cave he could see a lightening of the sky, dawn was approaching. He moved cautiously to the cave opening and peered through. Too far away to see much detail, he was nevertheless able to see the smoke still drifting from the fires and that no buildings remained intact. It was too dangerous for him to investigate further; his compassionate soul wished to see if he could help but his gut shrivelled and shrank with fear at the thought of the soldiers. Whimpering, he spotted the travel pack he had dropped in his hurry to find sanctuary in the cave the previous night. As quickly as he could, he ran out, retrieved the pack and scurried back to safety.

Back in the cave he ferreted through his meagre belongings until he found the stoppered clay jar he used to carry clean water; a few deep gulps helped wash away the lingering taste of sickness. He also found some slightly wizened apples and a dried-out hunk of cheese. He nibbled cautiously – the food stayed down so he ate a little more and pondered his options. There were few, he decided. Stay here in this cave until the soldiers left, or head to the village and confront the destroyers. Only one of those choices gave him some hope of survival.

As it turned out, he didn't have long to wait for them to go. Later that same day, once they were sure they had plundered anything of value, they left carrying the spoils with them. At the head of the short procession was the tall, bearded man who had orchestrated the blood eagle torture.

The prophet waited for several more hours before venturing into what had once been a bustling small village of around 100 people. What he saw made the sour apple and hard cheese he'd eaten earlier roil and churn in his stomach. Not one of the wooden buildings remained upright, most showed signs of fire damage. Villagers were strewn around in pools of blood, some missing limbs, some decapitated; all mutilated – even the smallest of the children. As he looked more closely he realised that all of them had had their hearts removed, he shook his head in sorrow...the heart was the seat of the soul, if it were missing in death then there could be no resurrection, no redemptions. The attackers had underlined their destructive capabilities by denying their victims a chance of an afterlife.

He became aware of a low buzz and realised with distaste that flies were already gathering around the pitiful remains of the villagers. He had to do something, he couldn't just leave them like this. As one man he couldn't hope to dig enough graves, but he could perhaps set a funeral pyre.

For the rest of that day and long into the night, he worked to bring all the shattered bodies into the centre of the village. Once that grisly task was accomplished he pulled the remnants of the wooden houses around the bodies, piling some on top too. He had decided it would take too long to build a pyre to put the people on, and hoped that creating a fire on top and around them would suffice. He stopped only when even the light of the moon was insufficient for him to see clearly, and curled up on the ground pulling a blanket he'd found over the top of him. As he'd gone about his work that day, he had realised the attackers had left a lot of the more mundane chattels behind, although nothing made of metal appeared to remain.

Sleep finally came upon him but he awoke with the first light of dawn and continued on his task, without recourse to food or drink, until he was satisfied. Taking one last walk around and collecting anything of potential use to himself, he eventually stopped in front of the makeshift funeral pyre and gave a eulogy for all those now lost. With his flint and iron, he lit a torch he'd found and touched it to the wood atop the bodies, and then in several places around the sides. For several moments nothing much seemed to happen, but the clothing of the people finally caught, and the fire took hold rapidly after that, pouring black oily smoke into the air.

But still the one known as prophet didn't rest. Instead he made his way down to the nearby river and submerged himself, robe and all, scrubbing and soaking in the icy water until he felt he had cleared the blood, muck and ash from himself. Emerging cold but cleansed he discarded the formerly white robe for one of the salvaged blankets and made his way slowly back to the sanctuary of his cave with the rest of the goods he'd found, the glow from the torch he had relit guiding his steps.

He could see the pyre from the cave, burning brightly, cleansing the despoiled village with flames and heat. By the light of the torch, he delved deep into his travel pack and extracted the writing materials he carried with him wherever he went…he may not be a soldier, may be unable to fight the evil that pervaded this place, but he could at least ensure the foul deeds were written down so that others would know the depravity of these invaders.

He smiled bitterly to himself, the villagers called him prophet, he had never corrected them, but he was no prophet, no man of God – no, he was a bard, a weaver of words, a storyteller and he would write the story of the barbarians and hope others would read them, take heed and flee, as far away as they could.

That would be his legacy.

Words.

26 May – prompt "It is simple," he said, looking towards her with a mix of confusion, frustration and for the love of God, an underlying current of lust

It's All Just Energy

"It is simple," he said, looking towards her with a mix of confusion, frustration and for the love of God, an underlying current of lust. Lust for the woman who had made him turn on his heels and pivot without thought, preparation or justification into an entirely new way of looking at the world. "Once I accept that everything is energy, then I have to admit that my life to date has been a lie!"

She looked at him with a degree of sympathy, she could remember how hard she had battled to understand and accept the concept. How she had struggled to reconcile that everything in life is mutable, because everything, including herself, was comprised of the same thing – energy – just vibrating at different frequencies.

"Mike, your life has never been a lie. You have lived as you saw fit for these last 38 years; would you berate a small child for not writing a novel when they haven't yet learned the alphabet? The key is, now that you do know, what will you do, will you change anything?"

The man sitting across the table from her put his head in his hands and sighed, "I have no idea. The concept feels so right and yet there is so much to take in."

"Take some time," she soothed, "this IS a huge reality switch for you. No need to try anything different just yet. I have given you the tools to question both yourself in this life and the many you have lived before. Explore, uncover, reveal and then release any and all negative thoughts, beliefs and patterns. Remember to replace anything you have negated with something positive and always, always look to be in flow."

He chuckled and shrugged his shoulders, "You make it all sound so easy Evie!"

"It is as easy, or as difficult as you choose to make it."

"Now you sound like bloody Yoda...do or do not, there is no try!"

That made both of them laugh and the palpable tension in the room was suddenly released, Mike felt it and raised a questioning eyebrow...

"Good, you felt it. Laughing and happiness are higher vibrational energies, our shared laughter energy has replaced the worry and confusion energy you were putting out."

Eve took his hand, "Mike, you have this, I wouldn't have even mentioned this to you if I didn't feel you could handle it. People are waking up all over the world and recognising that there is more to living than consuming more and more...It will be our time soon; we need to be ready."

Tension released, the pair made more coffee and, at least for a while, switched their conversation to less intense matters. Inevitably though they eventually reverted to their original topic...it was not so much a single elephant in the room as a full herd, and as such could not be ignored.

"How did you first realise the energy thing?" Mike quizzed.

"Serendipity, I think," Eve laughed. "A bit like you, I'd been unhappy with...well, with everything, for a long time. I kept changing stuff...jobs, men, where I lived, colour of my hair...anything to see if I could figure out what was keeping me back. I just *knew* there was more to existence than birth – life – death, and I knew I was destined for something...I just didn't know what!" Pausing, she took a long drink of her coffee. "One day I was twatting around on social media when I saw an advert for an 'energy conference' and it caught my attention. Before I knew what had happened, I'd clicked the link and bought a three-day ticket!"

"Energy conference?! I'd have been worried I'd booked on EON's annual works do!"

"Ha ha, very funny! Anyway, the rest, as they say is history. I attended the course, it sparked something deep inside me which led to me retraining as a therapist...and thus to meeting you. Something I am very, very grateful for because you have taught me something, well perhaps reminded me would be a better description."

Mike looked puzzled. "What are you talking about Eve, you're the therapist, you're the one who has helped me?"

"We learn something from everyone we meet Mike, we exchange energy all the time. When we first started messaging online, I remembered just how much I love words and how much I love writing stories. It was you that gave me the idea to write a book about energy after you mentioned The Celestine Prophecy – a book I'd forgotten about because..."

"The movie was so bad!" Mike finished the sentence for her.

"Indeed!" Eve snorted with laughter. "But don't you see, if you hadn't mentioned that, and you hadn't told me you were in publishing then writing this book would never have come about." She indicated the pile of neatly typed A4 sheets on the table. "Everything for a reason, remember?"

He nodded. "When you first sent me your manuscript, do you know what I thought?" Eve shook her head. "I though, oh crap, here we go again, another wannabee author with no discernible talent! How wrong was I though? 'All Things Being Equal' blew me away – I was hooked within the first chapter and I can't remember the last time that happened to me."

Eve blushed deeply.

"Add to that the whole, 'we are all energy', and I found myself having to reassess my own life...you have totally shaken up everything I thought I knew about myself – including my previous propensity for small, blonde women." He cast the tall, willowy, dark haired woman a meaningful look, causing her to blush even more deeply. "Eve, I think we could do great things together with your book, I want to publish it. I want to get your message out there; everyone needs to hear it. Plus, it will make a much better movie than The Celestine Prophecy!"

This made them both laugh again. "But there's another thing Eve – I think WE would be great together if we gave ourselves a chance. Bugger the therapist, patient thing, we are WAY past that. What do you say?"

Eve pushed a strand of dark wavy hair behind her ear. "I think that our entire lives have been leading to this. We're from different parts of the world, different cultures, different upbringings...but together we are more than the sum of just the two of us. So yes, we deserve a chance."

The pair stood then and embraced, third eye to third eye. Their aura's intertwined and intermingled, producing a discernible golden glow – a halo – around them. As they kissed for the first time the glow increased in size, expanding and embracing everything around them, growing...growing...growing.

Everything is energy.

Everything is love.

27 May from a prompt "despite there being more traffic than they'd ever seen"

Looking Ahead

Despite there being more traffic than they'd ever seen, they managed to get to the airport in advance of the obligatory 10-hour check in. On the drive in they'd reminisced about the 'good old days', when check-in was 2 hours and you were able to drop your baggage at automated check-in desks.

"None of that now," Nigel had moaned. "It almost doesn't seem worth going anywhere these days with all this bloody malarkey!"

"Well you're the one wanted to go to Fuengirola again, Nigel! I'd have been perfectly happy with a couple of weeks in Bognor, but oh no! You being Bertie Big Bollocks after that lottery win have to splash the cash."

Nigel's wife Sharon had never been particularly impressed with holidaying abroad, on account of the fact that she was a fussy eater and not one for sunbathing. She had acceded to his wishes for "one last trip" because he'd promised '5 Star all the way, none of that cheap all-inclusive stuff this time Shaz" What he'd neglected to tell her, probably because he hadn't found out until after he'd booked, was that post Covid 33 the travel industry had changed...a lot.

After the first few strains of the novel Covid virus; that is from 2020 to 2029; the world had picked itself up and just carried on; sure there were a few changes, face masks for instance became compulsory for everyone outside of their own homes from 2026, but holidays and travel, although more expensive, were largely unchanged.

2030 however saw 'THE BIG ONE', the global pandemic to top every global pandemic (except perhaps bubonic plague in the 14th century) and 65% of the world population succumbed. It made the outbreak in 2020 look like comparing fisticuffs to nuclear warfare. Everything had to change after that; travel was possible, but you had to really, really want to and every step of the way was regimented. Large travel companies and tour operators became a thing of the past as holidays fell under state control.

By some miracle Sharon and Nigel, despite being in their 60s when Covid first hit the headlines in 2020, had managed to survive each and every pandemic. Sharon had been seriously unwell in the 2022 outbreak and Nigel in 2026 but they'd each pulled through and now thought of themselves as invincible.

The lottery win, when they had both just retired aged 75, had been a bit of a bonus and they'd been able to (in Sharon's words) "have a bit of work done". As a consequence, despite now having reached the grand old age of 90, each of them was nipped and tucked as tight as a 30-year-old and

Sharon admitted to having no feeling in her face at all due to the vast amounts of Botox she'd had. Nigel still retained a bit of facial flexibility, but his skin was the colour of an antique mahogany table thanks to the large doses of tanning pills.

Arriving at their designated parking booth at the airport, their autodrive vehicle had docked efficiently at the first quarantine stop. They held their travel documents in front of a lens which appeared outside the triple glazed side windows and received the 'green' OK response. First stage passed.

The second stage involved them pressing their inner wrists to the same spot so their combined health insurance and health status details could be read from the implants just under their skin. Again, 'green' for OK. All that remained now was for them to stay in the vehicle for a further three hours whilst fresh air containing broad spectrum antivirals, antibiotics and a type of disinfectant suitable for human consumption was pumped into the cabin.

Sharon sniffed suspiciously, "Smells like the horrid stuff they used to use in schools back in the day."

"Well it's what has to happen so put up with it,

woman, another three hours of it yet."

Nigel rested his head back, shut his eyes and was soon snoring gently. Sharon snorted in disbelief, but tried to the same thing, only to be stymied by the fact that the skin on her neck was now so tight that she couldn't in fact tip her head back. Still she managed to rest her head against the side of the cabin and snooze a little like that.

The shrill noise alerting them to the end of stage one quarantine jarred them both from their slumber and the vehicle began to move further into the airport. At the next stop their baggage was removed from the rear of the car, taken to a holding area and thoroughly disinfected; and there it waited, swabbed and tested every hour, until being loaded on their plane. The couple had to remain in the cabin for a further two hours, but a complementary tray of drinks and nibbles was passed, via robotic arm, through a window which automatically slid down and back up again.

Sipping on her Mojito, Sharon remarked that she'd need the facilities if she were to drink much more. The vehicle's onboard AI overheard her and a plastic 'She Wee' complete with tube which passed into the floor, appeared from a concealed panel. This caused Nigel to laugh so hard that his toupee started to slide, which would have made Sharon laugh, if of course she were able to move her face.

Finally, the couple's vehicle docked at their departure bay and they were allowed out into a self-contained and sealed room. To one side was a bathroom and on another was a large view screen and a terminal to allow them to browse and make purchases from the duty-free selection which would then be waiting for them upon their arrival at the 5 Star hotel in Fuengirola. There were a couple of very comfortable reclining chairs and a unit dispensing food and drink.

The next few hours passed rapidly enough, and they received the news that they and their luggage had been pronounced Covid clear and could therefore board the plane.

"Please take your seats, fasten the safety belts and we will board you now," a disembodied voice came into the cabin. Sitting in the comfy chairs, they were aware of a sense of movement but with no exterior window they couldn't see a thing.

"Bloody odd, this," grumbled Nigel.

"You should have asked a few more questions then, shouldn't you! Wasted a whole day so far!"

A solid thunking noise interrupted the incipient disagreement and a message flashed on the view screen. "YOU ARE NOW ABOARD FLIGHT 732 TO MALAGA. ENJOY YOUR FLIGHT".

"Ooh, Nigel, I didn't realise we stayed in here the whole time, you're right this is bloody weird!"

Two and a half hours later they were disembarked, still in the same 'pod' and never having had a glimpse out of a window. They were transported to a docking area and thence to an automated vehicle which took them to their hotel.

Looking out of the window, Nigel couldn't see anything he recalled from previous visits 40 odd years ago. Gone was anything that would distinguish the area from any other hot place in the world, any quaintness, any Spanishness had been subsumed by globalism. The vehicle took them directly to their suite at the hotel, docking directly into it in fact, and the couple alighted into a sumptuous room with a sea view and a small private pool. Their luggage was waiting for them.

"What d'ya think then Shaz? 5 star or what?"

"Very nice – and it's just as well as it looks like this is it for the next couple of weeks!"

"What do you mean, I've got all sorts of things planned for us to do!"

Sharon simply pointed to a notice on a screen in front of them which read,

'Welcome to Hotel International Fuengirola. You are reminded that leaving the environs of your suite, pool and private beach area are strictly forbidden under Global Pandemic Law. We hope you enjoy your stay with us!'

28 May from a prompt "as the winds of change swept through the world"

A Parable for our Times

As the winds of change swept through the world everyone, in their own way, had a part to play in what was to come. Every action, no matter how small and insignificant it may have seemed at the time, could have had a profound effect on the ultimate outcome...we would all do well to remember that.

The first rumblings of change had been felt several generations earlier when female emancipation had, for want of a better phrase, 'taken off'. It was a long slow struggle, the old guard resisted, as you would expect, but the divine feminine worked quietly, resolutely, in the background; changing mindsets, changing beliefs and ultimately giving women equal rights – in the eyes of the law at least.

At the same time the drive for racial equality took hold; and disability, gay, lesbian, transgender rights...it seemed as though the world was finally going to become a fairer place for all humans.

The dark, the old paradigm, the ancient masculine, who revelled only in power and subjugation and who had led humanity for thousands of years, felt his power shrinking; felt his influence waning and he wasn't happy...he wasn't happy at all!

He whispered quietly in the ears of disaffected men, and women, reminding them of 'the glory days' when they could take whatever they wanted from whomever they wished; with impunity and with little fear of retribution or punishment. Some heard his whisperings and harked back to those days; they elected politicians and governments who matched those old systems and then expressed surprise when only a few; a very few; benefited.

Yet still they didn't learn, he wouldn't let them. "It's not your fault," he said quietly, insidiously, "it's the immigrants, the gays, the lesbians, the crippled, the poor, the clever women, the different. They don't know their places anymore."

They nodded, agreeing with the small dark voice that lived inside them; they had to try harder, fight back, show these people where they belong.

Even more strident politicians and governments were elected, taking ever more power into their greedy hands, stripping back rights and persuading those who could be persuaded 'that it was all for their own good'. And the people fell for the lies, no matter what wrong was done, they believed it was for their own good.

Yet the divine feminine, the mother, the Yin to the masculine Yang - Gaia; never gave up. She worked on assiduously, spreading her mantra of love, equality and flow. Her voice could be heard in the quietness of an early morning and the calm of dusk – at least for those open to hear it. Her colours glowed in all the flowers throughout the world and in her messengers, the butterflies. Stay strong. Stay calm. Love. Beauty. Balance. Peace.

In one last desperate push to maintain his stronghold in the world, the ancient masculine began to openly manipulate his puppets, speaking directly through them, directing policies and bringing together power cabals that would take over the world under the guise of 'business'. Those that resisted found themselves removed from office, or positions of power and his mannequins were put in place.

Gentle souls learned to stay away from the offices of government but that didn't mean they did nothing. Instead of outright, visible actions, they adopted the way of the mother and quietly began to rebuild society in individual suburbs, towns and villages. They planted and grew their own food, raised livestock. Taught their children the value of compassion, of care of collaboration, of respecting the world and everything in it.

The madness raged all around them, disease, aggression, monetary collapse, hyper-inflation...WAR. But Gaia protected them, kept them safe, helped them grow, evolve; prepared them for the time yet to come.

Eventually the ancient masculine grew weary, no matter what he did he could not get back the old ways. He could feel the warmth and love of the divine feminine and a part of him...a tiny part at first...began to yearn for her.

The mother smiled and continued to do what she had always done.

The light began to grow within the ancient masculine; the cold hardness of his heart began to soften and warm; he lost all interest in controlling, in ruling and his puppet governments and armies collapsed, their strings cut.

"Mother! Gaia!" he called. "I am sorry. Please let me return to you."

"You never left me child," she said, in a voice as smooth and sweet as the finest honey. "You simply lost your way for a while, as all children do."

The ancient masculine was thus reunited with his mother Gaia and a new golden age began for those of Earth's children who still remained.

29 May from a prompt "looking back to the future and on to beyond"

Dystopia Falling

"And as we reflect on what has passed and what is yet to come, we are looking back to the future and on to beyond."

The speech finished to rapturous applause, but Jenny turned to her companion and whispered. "What does that even mean? It's nonsense, a sound bite for a self-obsessed audience from a self-indulgent orator. Let's get the hell out of here."

She grabbed Robin's hand and the two of them began to make their way out of the auditorium. It was slow progress trying to push between the crowds of obsequious followers and they attracted a great deal of attention; no one was supposed to leave at this stage – this was the part where party loyalty was expected to be demonstrated.

Finally, they reached one of the exits out onto the drab grey street. It had been raining, and greasy looking puddles dotted the paving slabs, settling in the hasty tarmac repairs ready to soak the unwary walker. Neon streetlamps cast a sickly light and drained any joy or colour from the environment. Jenny shivered and pulled the collar of her coat up, trying to bury her head into its warmth.

Catching sight of this, Robin smiled, "You look like a tortoise trying to get its head back in its shell!"

Jenny laughed, "Aye? Well I feel more like a bloody mushroom than a tortoise! How can people believe the shit we are fed day in and day out? Not only believe it but applaud it, beg for more, hero worship the arse-wipes who feed it to us. I don't understand Robin, I really don't, and I don't think I want to be here anymore!"

Robin looked around nervously, "Shush Jen, someone might hear you!"

"And what if they do? What could they do? As far as I'm aware, free speech is still part of the law of this land. SHIT!" Jenny stopped in her tracks, she'd stepped in one of the puddles and the heel of her shoe had wedged into a crack in the paving and remained there whilst her stockinged foot had landed in the water. She hopped on one foot not wanting to put her unshod foot down again. "Robin, see if you can pull my shoe out."

He was already tugging gently at the shoe, but it wasn't loosening, the heel was really wedged in. Gentle wiggling didn't help either, so he yanked harder and came away with the shoe in his hand; the heel however was still stuck in the crack.

"Fuck! That was my only decent pair of shoes!" Jenny exclaimed. "Ah sod it!" She took the heelless shoe from Robin's hand, put it on and began to walk away.

Her uneven gait as she attempted to march off made Robin want to laugh. He could feel the bubbles of laughter rising but quickly supressed them, now was not the moment. Later he could recount the story and she would giggle along with him; right now, she was too angry, too righteous, for humour. With a final tug he managed to remove the heel from its concrete fixing and hurried after her.

"I'm not sure if it's fixable, not being an expert on ladies' shoes, but here's the heel."

Jenny took it from his outstretched hand and for a moment seem poised to lob the broken thing into the distance, before thinking better of it and dropping it into her coat pocket.

"Sorry Robin, you know how this all winds me up." She waved her arms as if to encompass everything. "Is it really us that is out of step with everyone else? Or are we right to believe that this whole world is right royally fucked up but no one else can see it? I just don't know any more and I so tired of constantly feeling as if I am battling against something I can't see but I know is there!"

He caught her by the shoulder and spun her round to face him. "Ah Jens, I don't think it's just us love. I do think some of us have caught on to what's happening sooner than others though and that's what causing this disconnect for us. You and I aren't alone, we know that, we see other people saying similar things every day."

"True! We also see lots of those people disappearing too. What happens to them?! No one in authority cares, no one looks for them. What if we're next?" Robin hugged her tight.

"We can't think like that. You and I just have to keep going. Keep doing what we're doing. Keep spreading the word. Keep pointing out the lies and the half-truths they feed the people. We know this world order is crumbling, we just have to prepare for the future."

Jenny hugged him back and they walked arm in arm to their small flat on the outskirts of the drab industrial town.

Back at the auditorium, the couple's early exit from the rally had been noticed and officials were studying the video of the pair of them as they fought their way through the crowds to the exit.

"Got them!" said a weasel-faced man with sharp features and thinning red hair. "Jenny and Robin Croft. She's a writer and he's an IT specialist. No known affiliation to the New Dawn party that I can see."

A rather more portly man peered over his shoulder. "Put them on the list and do some more digging. Something about them I don't like."

The other man sighed, Rogers didn't appear to like anyone if the truth be known, but he dutifully added the couple's names to the ever-growing dissident list. Doubtless they would be rounded up and 'disappeared' as had so many before them; although the country's leaders repeatedly denied this was happening.

The following morning, Jenny and Robin were working diligently on their respective projects; he from a small office space they had created in a spare bedroom and she from the living room, laptop balanced on her knee. They had fallen into an easy routine; they'd both get up around 8 a.m. and share tea and toast whilst watching the news for half an hour or so. By 9 a.m. Robin would be logged onto his system whilst Jenny would have begun working on the novel she was writing – an allegorical story of the current political situation. Their days passed in the kind of contentment neither had experienced back when they had each individually commuted to jobs they loathed.

Back at the Party HQ, Rogers was trawling through data lifted from personal online accounts.

"Jackpot!" he said aloud. "Jennifer Croft, author of the dystopian series of books 'New Dawn Coming'. That's close enough for me!"

Picking up his desk phone he swiftly arranged for the special task force to mobilise and arrest the couple. These ones were not getting away!

At around midday, Robin ambled into the living room where Jenny, far from typing furiously as he'd expected, was sitting quietly, concentrating. "Can you hear that?" she asked, noticing he had appeared. "Kind of a really low thrum."

Robin tilted his head on one side. "Now you've said it, yes I can. I can also hear sirens; some poor sod is doubtless going to be 'disappeared'."

The thrumming abruptly stopped, making the sound of the sirens, which were very near now, even louder. The small living room was suddenly flooded with a bright, bright golden light and, just as the front door was kicked inwards, the couple disappeared. Literally disappeared into thin air.

Running into the room the lead officer shouted, "Hands in the air!" but his words met an empty space. Jenny's laptop lay on the floor as if just dislodged from her knees, and of the couple there was no sign. "Check the rest of the house." It didn't take long – there was no sign of either of them.

"Christ Alfeckinmighty! Again! Have we actually managed to bring anyone on that list in yet?" one of the men asked.

The leader was already reporting back to HQ; despite numerous attempts, not one of the people they had been sent to collect had ever been arrested...not one of them had been where they were supposed to be and not one had ever been found since. It was a mystery!

Meanwhile, a very shocked but extremely grateful Jenny and Robin were being introduced to a host of other dissidents and New Dawn members aboard a huge alien spacecraft which, according to their rescuers, had been orbiting the planet for years evacuating people at risk of persecution by the old order.

"Their time is fading; this is their last desperate bid to hang on to the dark. We are simply holding the light, and light beings like yourselves, until it is safe for you to return and reclaim your world."

This was the only explanation they had received from the tall, golden woman who had greeted them, but it was all they had needed because in their hearts they already knew.

30 May from a prompt "As the ice began to melt a knife began to appear"

Expect the Unexpected

As the ice started to melt a knife began to appear. Judd, the archaeologist in charge of this particular dig in the Siberian permafrost, looked more closely. Only the top couple of centimetres of the hilt was visible; what little he could see looked to be finely made, there was even evidence of decoration.

His eyes furrowed in concentration and the twin lines between his brows became even more prominent than usual. When this anomalous chunk of ice had been excavated from the permafrost around Lake Baikal, Siberia, no one had any idea what was hidden inside. Or even what the large block of ice was doing several metres away from the lake and at a depth of 15 metres.

Judd enjoyed mysteries, he had been drawn towards archaeology from a young age, inspired (if he was honest) by the Indiana Jones films he watched as a kid. He'd run digs in this part of Siberia before; Lake Baikal, being the oldest and deepest freshwater lake in the world, held a special fascination for him. So large it could be mistaken for a sea and at least 25 million years old, Judd was convinced there were ancients secrets connected to this area. He and his team had uncovered evidence of human habitation dating back to the Palaeolithic, but he was convinced this unique area was holding secrets far more interesting than the detritus of seal hunters and fishermen.

"Hey Judd!" a voice called, jolting him out of his reverie. "Anything interesting happening with that ice block yet?"

"Not unless you call evidence of a tooled knife

interesting. You made me jump by the way! Nearly cracked my head on the heat lamp." Judd turned to face the owner of the voice, his second in command and also his long-term partner, Sarah.

Sarah's eyes had opened wide at the mention of the word knife and she hurried across to his side. Despite the aforementioned heat lamp, the room they were in was barely above freezing point and she, like he, wore a heavy parka and gloves. Bundled up as she was, Sarah still presented an attractive picture; 5' 9" and slender, with dark wavy hair and brown eyes. Even after 10 years together, Judd remained surprised that she had ever agreed to go out with him in the first place.

"Knife?! Did you say knife?"

He nodded, "See."

"Oh my goodness! That's amazing, look at the detail!" She peered in closer. "I wonder what else this block is concealing. Is there any way to speed up the thaw?" Even as she said it, Sarah was aware that there wasn't. It had to be a slow process in order not to subject whatever was in there, if indeed there was anything in there, to extreme temperature change.

Judd shook his head, "You know there isn't love. Not that I don't wish there was! Let's set up some cameras around the ice. At least while we aren't here we can record the melt and not miss a thing."

It took a matter of minutes to encircle the block; which was approximately 3 metres long by 1.5 metres wide; with 6 cameras, all linked to the internal computer network so they would be able to view from any location in the camp.

"Job's a goodun. Is there any food on offer?" Judd was renowned for several things – one having a bottomless pit of an appetite.

"That was what I was coming to tell you before you distracted me with your magically emerging knife...which sounds a bit like a crap euphemism doesn't it?!" She giggled. "Andy's made a kind of stew with some canned veg and the meat those local traders gave us. I've not tried it, but it smells pretty tempting."

"YOU smell pretty tempting," Judd responded, grabbing her around the waist, "and you can watch my magically emerging knife anytime you like."

Sarah laughed and kissed him, "Come on, Indy, time to eat, you need to keep your strength up, man!" She pulled free from his embrace and ran to the door, giggling as he chased after her.

The pair arrived in the mess hall and collapsed in helpless laughter onto the nearest bench seat. The other team members, well used to the antics of their leader and second in command, barely raised an eyebrow between them and simply waited for their hysteria to calm.

It was much warmer in the mess hall and everyone was in jeans and t-shirts; Sarah and Judd, already warmed by the chase through the compound, quickly shed their outerwear.

"You two ready for some grub?" a small blonde man with a goatee beard asked.

"Please Andy. Have you worked out what the meat is yet?" Sarah asked.

"Nope, not a clue but it tastes good!"

Two large bowls of the steaming stew were plonked down in front of them, together with some hunks of bread from a loaf which had been defrosted from their now dwindling stocks of food. They set at the food with gusto, the lower temperatures of the area and the physically demanding work meant they burned through calories more rapidly than if they were desk-based.

Reaching the end of his bowl, Judd mopped up the remnants with his last bit of bread, "Now that was pretty damn good! I don't suppose…"

"There's anymore?" Andy interrupted already putting another full bowl and fresh piece of bread in front of him. "Knock yourself out mate."

Once Judd had finally finished eating, the entire team gathered together to discuss the day's finds and plan tomorrow's schedule. Neither Judd nor Sarah mentioned the progress with thawing out the ice block until they were sure everyone else had had their say. Casting a glance his way, and receiving an imperceptible nod in return, Sarah made the announcement of Judd's discovery.

It was no surprise that the entire team wanted to head down to the cold store to take a look, but Judd persuaded them otherwise. He opened a nearby laptop and pressed a few keys, "Switch on the big screen someone."

Six images appeared on the large screen, each a view of the ice block from a different angle; including one from directly above. The third picture clearly showed something emerging from the ice and Judd clicked to bring that to full screen size.

"Wowser!" one of the younger men exclaimed. "How cool is this?"

The group gathered around the screen, throwing questions at both Judd and Sarah; chief amongst which was how long the block would take to melt completely.

"At least another 48 hours I would estimate," Judd replied.

There were groans all around.

"At least we can watch the progress in here where it's warm," Sarah laughed, "it's only a notch above freezing in that cold store you know!"

For the next couple of hours, before they all disappeared off to their comfortable but basic quarters, the team speculated as to the contents of the block and the origins of the knife. The ideas ranged from Neolithic hunter with a flint knife, to the more outlandish traveller from the future trapped in a sudden change of temperature. There was a great deal of laughter at this bizarre suggestion and the team headed for bed in good spirits.

Over the course of the next two days everyone stared at the screen whenever their other duties permitted. The melt was agonisingly slow, imagine defrosting a freezer in a garage where the temperature never gets above 2 degrees and you'll have some idea, but by noon on day two most of the hilt of the knife was visible and it was like nothing any of them had seen before.

Perfectly preserved, what looked like writing, but in a language none of them knew, spiralled around the hilt. From the screen it was almost impossible to tell what the material was, and the blade was still not visible. Nothing below the level of what appeared to be a guard had yet thawed out. Judd stared quizzically at the screen, the fact that some kind of guard was visible on the knife was jarring with him...it was too modern and made no sense.

It was the morning of the third day before the ice revealed its secret and it was not what any of them could have expected.

"Judd!" Sarah bellowed from the mess hall at 6 a.m. on that third morning. "JUDD!"

He came flying in, hair stuck up all over the place and wearing only pyjama bottoms. Sarah was staring transfixed at the screen; as Judd got closer his jaw dropped…

"Holy mother of God, what the hell is that?"

"I have no idea, none whatsoever. I've honestly only ever seen anything like it in a movie before."

On the screen in front of them was displayed a body, intact and in perfect condition, the ice having preserved it well. The body was slender, dressed in a tight-fitting suit of some sort. Long thin hands, each with only three fingers, were clasped around the visible part of the blade of the knife, or more accurately dagger. The rest of the blade clearly penetrated the thin chest. Most shocking of all was the head; large, bulbous, with no nose, a mere gash where a mouth should be and pale grey coloured skin.

What had they found?

31 May – an idea for a future novel

A Slip in Time

I find it hard to believe that more than 80 years have passed since I first 'discovered' my unusual gift, and it is a gift; despite all the confusion it has caused in my life, all the hiding, lying and pretence, I wouldn't change a single thing.

It was November 1939, war had been declared in the September but nothing much had happened...in fact I had heard the adults around me refer to this period as the phoney war.

At the age of 12 and a half I was just beginning to show the outward signs of approaching puberty, my breasts were (as mother said) 'budding' and I had found a few dark silky hairs in my armpits and around my groin. I was though, still very much a child, with childish thoughts, so it came as something of a shock when a lad on the tram from the city centre to home wolf-whistled and proceeded to follow me after I alighted. He was several years older than I – perhaps 17 or 18, wearing shabby clothes and a flat cap, and not someone I recognised. I could however recall having seen him at the tram stop – had he followed me?

He tried to engage me in conversation.

I pointedly ignored him.

He persisted, eventually grabbling my arm just as I turned onto my street.

'Stuck up bitch...think you're so much better than me, do you?'

My heart was thumping uncomfortably in my chest, my hands were sweating, and I longed to run for the safety of home – but it was still some distance to my house, and he was bigger, stronger and undoubtedly faster than me.

I didn't know what to do. Nothing in my short life had prepared me for such unpleasantness and so I turned to face him, intending to insist that he leave me alone. The young man however took my movement as an opportunity to pull me towards him and force a kiss on me.

I could taste the beer he must have been drinking, the cigarettes he had smoked; and I could smell a sour, rank odour of stale perspiration. Crushing me against his bony chest he tried to force his tongue into my mouth whilst one hand pressed into the small of my back and the other grasped my buttocks.

Gagging, I tried to pull away. Tried to scream. But I couldn't break free. In my mind I shouted, 'LET GO' and wished fervently for him to disappear...

All of a sudden I pitched forwards, the tight embrace and groping hands no longer there...

Crying out with relief, I turned to head towards my

house...but everything was different. Instead of the row of terraced houses there was a dirt path, lined with mature trees. The air smelled clean, not thick with the scent of smoke from coal fires, and it was quiet...eerily so.

I shook my head, hoping to clear the vision. Opened and closed my eyes several times, but still the path, the trees, the fresh air and quietness remained.

Nonplussed, I looked every which way but could see no signs of habitation.

By now I was very close to tears and shaking like a leaf; spotting a moss-covered tree stump I sat down, head in hands, trying to work out what had happened and where I was. The sharp sound of a twig cracking as if it had been stood on, roused me from my reverie and panicked, I jumped up and ran into the trees at the side of the path.

Peering round the trunk of a large oak tree, I watched a group of people walking along the path. They were dressed simply but warmly, their clothing unfamiliar in style to me and they were chattering amongst themselves. As they grew closer, I realised I could understand their words but not the topic of the conversation.

A girl with dark hair, partially covered by a bright red knitted cap, was chatting animatedly to an older man – perhaps her father...

"Why do we have to work for the Baron?" she was asking. "Surely it would be better if we were allowed to have our own land."

The older man was looking around furtively. "Shush, child! That kind of talk could get you arrested! It's the way it has been for hundreds of years – the nobles own the land, all of the land, at the behest of the King, and we commoners have to work it. Nowt we can do to change what has always been!"

The girl looked angry. "That's *why* nothing changes, everyone just accepts that this is the way things are and will always be! I don't see why we can't do something about it! I heard that there have been some people across the great ridge as have been protesting. And Markus told me he's seen some London newssheet telling of clashes outside parliament."

The older man was beginning to look decidedly uneasy, he was glancing from side to side and shaking his head. "Marissa, stop! If anyone overhears you..." His voice tailed away as with a backwards jerk of his head he appeared to imply that those following on behind could have heard her comments.

The girl simply smiled broadly, "There's many of us young folk feel the same way, none here would disagree with anything I've said."

That statement appeared to upset the man even further. "You've talked widely about such things? Oh Marissa, how could you? You are my only child, my only blood relative – I cannot lose you the way I lost your brother and mother!"

"Mother was betrayed, Jon tried to save her! They both believed that change is overdue. If I am taken, then so be it...I would rather become a martyr to our cause than to continue to live at the beck and call of this corrupt ruling class!"

The older man looked truly horrified.

At that moment I slightly shifted my position behind the tree, the better to see the interaction, and in doing so I trod on a brittle fallen branch which snapped under my weight, causing a loud 'crack'.

All heads spun towards my hiding spot – I held my breath, fearing my breathing would give me away.

A squirrel suddenly appeared nearby; spotting the group of people, it made a beeline for the tree in front of me and shot up the thick trunk into the branches above.

The girl, Marissa, laughed loudly. "We're even frightened of squirrels! That's what happens living the way we do."

There was a collective sigh of relief and the party continued on their way, but not before I'd had a chance to clearly see Marissa's face – it was like looking in a mirror!

The air around me seemed to shimmer and without warning I found myself back in more familiar surroundings, the terraced houses of my home street. There was no sign of the youth who had assaulted me, but I noticed a flat cap on the ground.

Confused and not a little scared, I ran as quickly as I could until I reached the perceived safety of the front door of my house. It was unlocked, as it usually was, and I ran inside heading directly for the scullery. Once there I stuck my head under the tap and proceeded to wash my face and repeatedly rinse out my mouth in order to get rid of the foul taste of second-hand beer and cigarettes.

"Is that you Mary?" Mother's voice called from upstairs. "You're a little later than I thought you'd be. There's some bread and a bit of cheese on the cellar head for your tea. I'm off to meet your dad at some kind of talk about the war effort."

Part of me was relieved that she was going out because I knew she would spot that something had happened and worm the truth out of me. Oddly, I wasn't so much concerned about telling her of the strange events I had witnessed so much as the fact that some lad I didn't know had kissed me. Another part of me dearly wanted to open up and tell her what had happened, just to hear her say everything would be alright.

I think I knew, deep down inside though, that everything was not alright, that everything was going to change, HAD changed, for me that afternoon...

ABOUT THE AUTHOR

Born and raised in Sheffield, Laura now lives in the Peak District with her partner. A writer from childhood it has taken her until her 6th decade to take the leap of faith into bringing her work into the public gaze.

Laura's first novel "A Time for Grace" encompassed her passion for history and the mysteries of time. This anthology allowed her to explore other favoured genres such as dystopian science fiction and the future of mankind.

WIth several ideas in development (including 'spin offs' from these short stories) expect more books from her in the near future.

For details of our other books, or to submit your own manuscript please visit

www.green-cat.co

Printed in Poland
by Amazon Fulfillment
Poland Sp. z o.o., Wrocław

65845632R00157